chapter one

F irst day of basketball tryouts. The gym smells like rotten socks and last year's sneakers. It'd be a fail, a colossal fail, to play D2 in Grade 8. I've *gotta* make Division 1 this year.

I'm warming up, doing some power crossovers, when Roy Williams struts up to me, steals my ball, slam-dunks it, then hangs off the rim for about an hour, doing chin-ups. Dunking is *so* not an option for me. I'm five foot, five inches—in my shoes. Roy's over six feet—in his sock feet—and he can palm the basketball. He seriously looks like a gorilla. Crazy long arms, probably from hanging off the rim, big ears, smucked nose, fat lips.

"Your turn, Blob." He laughs and drills the ball at me, driving my middle finger back so it cracks. I bite my lip and try not to let on that it kills.

"It's Bob." My teeth are jammed together so tight I can hardly spit the words out. Like, Roy's a rusty nail giving me lockjaw. And doesn't he know that blobs are fat? I admit I used to be a little pudgy, before I lost my baby fat, but now I'm scrawny—James calls me "Stick-boy." He's just trying to be funny ... I think ... and he doesn't say it in public. For a totally cool, hardcore basketball god brother with a hot girlfriend, a 95 average, and a bazillion friends, James is okay.

Not like Roy. I can smell him following me around the gym. He wears this crazy aftershave even though he's still a baby-face like me. He smells like a Christmas tree, or cough drops. I try to ignore his shiny red basketball shoes squeaking along behind me. Seems he's got a new pair every month, probably five-toe discount. You know, walk in with the old, out with the new. I'm wearing my dad's vintage high-top black Chucks. Dad was a basketball phenom in school—MVP, Athlete of the Year material. Or at least he was, until he had to drop out to go to work. He's still the single-game scoring record holder at Oakdale High. His 1982 sneakers are only a bit too big for me—this year. Last year they were flipping off me. Roy's nickname for me then was "Bozo." How clever is that?

"So, Blob, what position you goin' out for this year—right or left bench?" Roy laughs—like some snorting pig. With his shaved head, he looks like a pig, too. Pig-gorilla combo: pigorilla. Last year, he made D1; I got cut in the second round and had to be a D2 loser. I keep my eyes on the net, fake right, then dribble left. Focusing on my ball handling's tricky when my shoulders keep getting closer and closer to my ears, like some turtle trying to hide in his shell. Why is this freakin' guy in my face all the time? What did I ever do to him? And why didn't he stay away when he left in Grade 3?

"Or, hey—you could be the geeky mascot, good old Oakley the Owl."

"Funny, Roy—you should be on the comedy channel." I try to sound tougher than I am. Only my voice cracks in the middle of "comedy." I cough and go in for a layup. He charges up behind me. Just as I'm going up, he stuffs me. Hard. My nose slams into his sweaty armpit, and my glasses fly into the end wall—with me right behind them. Just like in the cartoons. Except this hurts. Not like in the cartoons. I pick up my glasses. One arm's dangling from the frame. My own arm, my shooting arm, doesn't feel so great either.

"Thanks a lot, Roy—you'll have to pay for these!" I want to shove them in his face and tell him where to go. Instead, I just mumble. He's busy looking around to see who saw the stuff.

"You're such a klutz." He slams me into the wall with one of his meaty shoulders. "Why don't you get one of those geeky nerd-bands to hold them onto your stupid fat head? It'd look sweet with those messed-up shoes." Apparently, he doesn't notice my head's about half the size of his. Or that my brain's twice as big.

Coach Adams comes out of his office just then, writing something on his clipboard. I hope it's a big black x beside Roy Williams's name. Or maybe PERMANENT DETENTION. I'd never put him on the team, no matter how tall he is or how many points he scores.

Coach blows the whistle and we start running laps. I'm tired before I even start.

chapter two

Wednesday morning, I sleep in. Stupid James knows he's supposed to get me up when he's got early practice. Today, he must've hopped in Mom's car and taken off, leaving me in la la land. *Idiot!* Now I'll miss band—again. Mrs. Archibald is going to kick my butt out.

One thing I'm pretty good at is music. Not that it's something to get pumped about at Oakdale Middle. Carrying a trombone case is about the same as having a big loser "L" stamped on your forehead. When I'm not there, the horn section blows. Hey, is that one of those pun things we learned about? Archie'll notice I'm missing right away, since nobody else on trombone can even read music.

I yank on yesterday's shorts and a clean T-shirt, do a quick sniff check, then put on extra deodorant. A splash of water on my face and I'm good to go.

"Hannah, get up." I'm whispering and brushing my teeth at the same time. I wipe a bit of toothpaste froth off her cheek. "We're late—hurry up!"

She jumps out of bed and gives me a big toothy smile. She's always smiley, bouncy like Tigger, over-the-top happy. The worst of it is she's not faking it. She's really that sweet, like cotton candy, to *everybody*, even the nose pickers in kindergarten. If she wasn't my sister, I'd call her a super butt-kisser.

I'm the stuck-in-the-middle kid—in between perfect King James and precious Princess Hannah.

"Thanks, Bobby." She doesn't even sound sleepy. "I guess James was too busy and forgot us again, huh?"

"He forgets we're alive most of the time. You've got two minutes to get ready." I go downstairs, slap together two peanut butter and grape jelly sandwiches, and stuff them into bags. No juice packs; water'll have to do.

I throw on my backpack, grab my hoodie from the rack, take an apple off the table, and toss one to her. "Let's go. We're gonna have to run."

She slides her arms into the sleeves of my old red soccer jacket, zips up her little monkey backpack, and follows me out the door. "Mom must've worked really, really late last night. Do you think Daddy had a good night?"

"I didn't hear her come in. Maybe they both slept all night—I wish."

My mom's a continuing care worker, a babysitter for old people. My dad's sick.

We get to the door just as the last buses are pulling out

of the parking lot. "Bye, Bobby." Hannah squeezes my arm. "Hope you have a super awesome day! See you later, alligator!"

I pull my arm away. "Bye, Hanny."

"Bobby!"

"Okay, okay. In a while, crocodile." When's she gonna outgrow that little-girl huggy thing? I am so not into PDA—girly Public Displays of Affection.

Crap—there's the first bell. I'm really late now. One more late slip and I'm in detention for the next tryout. I slide through the door just as Andrews is about to close it. I don't think he likes me—probably because I'm no James, the Wonder Boy.

"Good morning, ladies and gentlemen—nice to see you all looking so bright-eyed and bushy-tailed this fine, sunny morning." Mr. Andrews strolls around the class with his hands behind his back, looking everybody over. Do we look like a bunch of squirrels? More like a bunch of slugs. He's the kind of teacher who always thinks he's hilarious. Doesn't seem to notice nobody's laughing. We're pretty sure he wears a wig—now that *is* funny. His hair's, like, dark brown and thick and curly—but he's about a hundred years old. Sometimes you can see the nasty gray hairs on the back of his neck, sproinging up over the collar of one of his collection of 300 or so plaid shirts.

Maria peeks in through the skinny window on the door. She knocks and he opens the door, just a crack, and lowers his face to the same level as hers.

"Sorry I'm late, sir," she whispers. "I promise it won't

happen again." Then she giggles. "At least, not this week."

Lucky for her, Andrews likes girls way better than boys. He doesn't even say anything about a late slip. Maria sort of reminds me of Hannah. She's friends with everybody—even the geeky kids and the ones that hide in the back corner of the cafeteria to eat lunch. She's cute, but not gorgeous; her hair's almost long enough to sit on. She mostly wears it in braids with different-colored ribbons on the ends. Most Grade 8 girls would be way too cool for that.

If I stop and think about it, Maria's the only girl I ever really talk to at school. Maybe I'm one of those geeky ones I was talking about. She's the only girl I know who plays the electric guitar. She's not bad; I mean, she's not into metal or anything, like me. But she's more real than lots of Grade 8 girls, if you know what I mean. Not all painted and ditzy, orange-tanned and stunned.

"Ahem—sorry to interrupt your deep pondering, Mr. Prescott—bottom of page 78, please and thank you."

"Sorry, Mr. Andrews ... right, page 78 ... got it." I better start listening up—I can just see the smoke blasting out of Coach's ears if Andrews gives me a detention. I've heard them going at it in the hall before, usually about some player missing practice time.

The thing I don't get is why stupid Roy and his Siamese twin Kyle never get detentions from Andrews. I'm guessing he likes them because they're basketball stars or something. Oh, yeah, and Jeff told me Andrews's wife is Roy's great-aunt; that might explain a few things. Like why Roy never gets his name on the board for being late and not doing his homework. Or skipping—he's always missing class. .

I put my head down and start working on the problems. Hey, there's a pun. What kind of teachers have lots of problems? Math teachers—especially Andrews. Math is pretty easy for me—by that I mean, it's *soooo* boring because Andrews teaches the same thing over and over. He sounds like the droids in those old Star Wars movies. How could anybody talk that much about numbers? I wish he'd come by and start teaching algebra some night when I can't sleep. I check the clock for the tenth time. Is it lunchtime yet?

chapter three

I sit in our usual back corner in the cafeteria, eating my PB & J slowly, hoping it'll fill me up. Seems like I'm always starving lately, waking up with a slimy pillow from drooly dreams about hamburgers and extra-cheese meat-lovers' pizza. Jeff and Andy are making up a science lab they missed last week, so I'm stuck eating alone. Loser with the ear buds. Mr. Invisible.

Back in nursery school, Jeff and me used to play superheroes; I was Mr. Invisible and he was SnapDragon, the Flame-Throwing Karate King. My best weapon was disappearing, which would be pretty sweet at Oakdale Middle School. On the bench, in the horn section, in boring math classes, when girls try to talk to me and I get all stuttery ...

"Okay if I sit here?" I look over my shoulder and see Maria

smiling down at me. Ribbons the same blue as her eyes today. I'm pretty sure my face is the same red as the apple on her tray.

I pull my buds out of my ears. "No, well ... I mean ... sure, whatever." I'm pretty smooth when it comes to talking to girls. By which I mean they make me crazy nervous, even Maria. I can't seem to look girls right in the eye. Boys are way easier. Mostly with my friends, we just grunt or burp. Talking's lame.

She unwraps her sandwich, then carefully folds up the waxed paper and puts it back in her lunch bag.

"So ... what's new?"

She's a vegetarian and eats some really moldy-looking stuff. It's usually green and nasty-looking—even the bread is all bumpy and lumpy, like something we'd put in the bird feeder. Actually, she kind of looks like a bird, all perky and fluttery. Sorta jumpy, but cute jumpy.

"New York, New Orleans," I say, without thinking.

She laughs.

I can feel the red creeping up my neck. "Crap. I sound like my dad."

"How is your dad?"

I drain my milk, squish the carton flat, and shrug. "Tired. Just finished chemo."

"Remember my Uncle Jack, the one that had the same kind of tumor a few years ago? His cancer's in remission; he's even back at work."

I shrug again and stuff a blue gummy worm in my mouth. Two years ago, Dad started losing his balance and falling down all the time. Turned out he's got a big nasty brain tumor, a C Monster Hannah calls it, near the base of his skull. Of course, it's in a place where they can't just dig it out, like the tumor Jeff's mom got cut out of her boob. How unfair is that?

"So, how're tryouts going?" Maria bites into a carrot stick dipped in peanut butter.

"About the same as last year. Brutal." I help myself to one of her carrots. "Roy busted my glasses yesterday. Gotta wait 'til I get paid Saturday to get them fixed."

"He is such a derp."

"Yeah. Makes the tryouts real interesting when I can't see the hoop. Or the ball, unless it's right in my hand."

She snaps a carrot stick in two. "His goal in life must be making everybody in the world feel like a pile of dog poop."

"He's doing a decent job, then," I say. "A real over-achiever." I start cleaning up my garbage. "I gotta go downtown, drop off my glasses, and pick up some drugs for my dad. Later ..."

"Want some company?" She stands up fast. Her T-shirt's got blue and pink owls all over it. "I could be your guide girl." She giggles. "Not the Girl Guides that sell cookies ... in case you can't see, I mean, like a guide dog."

"Sure ... I guess so." I've never actually walked anywhere with a girl before—except Hannah. It feels kind of weird—what'll we talk about? I hold the cafeteria door open for her—Mom would be so proud—and try to put a silencer on the apple belch that's brewing in my throat. Feels like a wet one, a vurp—part vomit, part burp.

Maria's one of the few Grade 8 girls I'm taller than, so

that's a good thing. The girls all turned into giants over the summer. The only thing giant about me is the zits all over my face. Oh, and my feet, I guess. Outside the band room, Roy's butting some Grade 6 boys at the water fountain. They've got that big-eyed puppy-in-the-headlights look. Lucky for them, Mrs. Archibald shows up. She grabs Roy by the ear, hard, and marches him to the back of the line, old-school style.

"Sweet." I don't realize I said it out loud until I notice the boys in the line staring at me. Some of them are grinning and laughing, but looking sideways at Roy at the same time. Roy's staring at all of us like he wants to rip our heads off, then slam-dunk them in the trash can.

"Chill," I say, giving the boys a big James smile. Maria laughs and we speed-walk out the main doors. I wonder if this would be considered a date, and if Roy's gonna kill me at tryout.

chapter four

"Hey, Blob ... who's the little girl I saw you with today?" Soon as I get to practice, Roy yells at me from the other side of the gym. "She one of your baby sister's friends? You robbin' the playpen?"

Like you're really interested. I dig through my bag like I'm busy looking for something and don't hear him. *Like, she's been in the same math class as you for six weeks, you moron.*

Coach makes us run twenty laps at the start of every practice. I'm in decent shape from running or biking out to work at Oaklawn Farm almost every day all summer. Joe, the guy who owns the farm, used to play ball with my dad, so he's teaching me a few of his tricks when we're not shoveling cow crap. Joe's a midget, like me, but he's fast for an old guy. We usually play to 21; in Grade 6, I used to get five, maybe six baskets. Sometimes he still wins, but mostly it's me now. He taught me my best shot—a reverse layup. I'm amazing at it in practice and one-on-one—but they're wicked hard to do in a game.

I finish my laps and grab a ball off the cart. Whoa! Is that my bicep? It's actually bigger than an egg. Come to think of it, I can't remember the last time James called me Stick-boy. When Coach handed out the practice jerseys yesterday, I needed a medium instead of small. At least I don't look so much like the team mascot anymore, especially without my glasses.

I'm halfway through my forty foul shots by the time Roy huffs and puffs his way to the line. Like the Big Bad Wolf and the Pillsbury Doughboy, all in one. He grew a little gut over the summer. In fact, he looks kinda puffy all over. Too many doughnuts and double-doubles, probably. I ignore him and keep shooting. I'm ten for twenty, which is way better than last year. The best NBA players shoot ninety percent from the free-throw line, so fifty percent isn't so bad.

You can learn a lot from watching the NBA on TV. One time, I saw this little guy—maybe an inch or so taller than me—win this mega slam-dunk contest. He won, like, a million bucks or something. Okay, maybe it was only a thousand. Anyway, his vertical jump was awesome. It's like he was defying gravity, like some astronaut. I've been working on my jump—sometimes I can touch the rim, just barely, with the tip of my middle finger.

I spin the ball, drive it into the floor, three solid bounces, then line it up with the net. BEEF: Balance, Eyes, Elbow, Follow-through. Swish! Roy's right behind me—air ball. I grab his "rebound" and sprint to the back of the line. Foul shots are the best—nobody defends on them. In a floor shot, you never know when you're gonna get an elbow to the head or your glasses knocked off. I like being on the line—foul shots are mostly the only points I get. Short guys like me get fouled lots.

Coach blows the silver train whistle he got when he retired from the railroad. "Okay, everybody in. Have a seat." We all sit on the bench and he paces up and down in front of us, looking at his clipboard. "Listen up, basketball players. You've got two more days to show me what you're made of. You need to be tough as nails, live to possess the ball. One team, one goal, no egos. The road to becoming a good basketball player is no cakewalk. It's paved with hard work, sweat, and ripped-up knees."

When he turns his back, I glance over at Jeff and Andy, then rub my knees.

"We're going to mix things up a bit today." Coach stops pacing and points at me. "Bob, you take Roy's position. Your ball handling's been looking good so far. Roy, I want you as post on the other scrimmage team. We could use a tall guy like you under the basket."

I put both hands under my jaw to keep it from hitting the floor. Seriously? I've wanted to play point guard since I started Pee Wee ball when I was four. Joe's been helping me with my ball handling—make like a monkey, he says. Keep low, bend your knees, and pretend the ball's on a tight elastic around your hand. Maybe the six billion hours I put in practicing over the summer will pay off this year. I wish.

I look over to see how Roy's taking the news. He's staring at me like he wants to slam-dunk my head again. His eyes are all slanty and his top lip's curled up on one side. Like a cobra. Great.

I carry the ball over half and look to set up a play. One thing I'm decent at is remembering plays. Plus, I can see the whole floor, even when I'm dribbling, usually. Today, everybody's a little blurry without my glasses. I think about driving to the hoop, but the key's full. No referee to count the three seconds, so everybody's living in the key. I do a bounce pass left to Jeff, and he passes it back out to me. Roy's busy staring at some girl walking by instead of playing defense. Here's my chance—I deke left, drive to the right, change hands, go in left, and there it is—a perfect reverse layup. Sweet! Nobody gets a piece of it. The other guys—well, everybody except Roy and Kyle—all hoot and high-five me.

"Nice move, Bob," Coach yells. "Just like the big leagues." I scratch my head where Roy's snake eyes are drilling into it, bend down, and pretend to tie my shoe. Don't want to look too happy—that'd really piss him off.

Second half of the scrimmage, Maria and her friends stop by to start decorating for the Halloween dance. I look over to check them out, which gives Kyle a chance to steal the ball and go end-to-end for a layup. Great.

"Keep your eyes on the ball, Prescott," Coach yells. "A guard has to see the whole floor *all* the time. Dig deep. Focus!"

I play a decent scrimmage. By which I mean I don't totally suck. Roy steals the ball from me three times, but I chase him down and manage to get it back once. Point guard's the position for me. Me and Steve Nash and Magic Johnson. I did a book report on Magic last year. He was a superstar guard until he retired and started raising money for AIDS charities; he's still a hero, but the kind that raises money now. An invisible hero.

"Not bad, Bobby," Coach says as we're all getting our stuff together. "Keep your head up and don't let them push you off the ball." I look up at him. He grins and gives me a wink. "Maybe we'll try you out in the pre-season game against Millwood next week."

"Thanks, Coach." I cram my gear into my gym bag and turn to leave. Does that mean he's gonna put me on the D1 team?

No time to dream. I've gotta hurry to pick up Hannah. I hear the squeaky shoes and smell him before I see him.

"Hey, Blob—you really sucked today. You're an idiot. You gotta be real smart to play guard." Roy shoves ahead of me and checks me with his super-size gym bag on the way out the door.

Why did he have to move back *here*? Why not Iceland, or maybe Africa? There's lots of tall people there. How about Darfur? Isn't there a war going on there?

"Coach is just being nice to you 'cause your brother was his star point guard."

"We'll see." I try to stay cool. "I'll let you know how much the glasses cost."

"Like I care." He slams down his skateboard and rides away.

I try to forget about him and think about the scrimmage. How great it felt controlling the play. But all I can think of is what he said about James.

chapter five

"We're home," Hannah calls out as the screen door bangs shut behind us. Mom's drying her hands on a dishtowel. She looks tired and real small, like Gram did before she died. I almost feel like giving her a hug, but Hannah does it for me.

"Pizza?" I give the air a big hungry sniff instead.

"Sorry—spaghetti again." Mom gives Hannah an extra-long hug, but she knows I'm past hugging. "Sauce made by Mr. Ragu."

"Sweet. I'm starved." I drop my backpack and gym bag in the hall. "Fifty pounds of homework in there. Should be illegal."

"How was the tryout?" Mom asks.

I shrug. "Eh. Not bad—got to play guard."

"That's nice, sweetie."

I never told her about my glasses the other day. Since I mostly only wear them for sports, maybe she won't notice. What I seriously don't want is her going to the principal about Roy. That would be instant social suicide. He's dangerous—and powerful, in a bad way.

"Hey, Dad." I stop by the living room on my way upstairs. "How are ya?" I pick through the candy in the bowl on the coffee table. He looks almost normal. Only he's wearing his orange bathrobe and it's five o'clock in the afternoon.

"I had a good day, a really good day." He turns off the TV. "Walked all the way to the post office. Then I met Joey for coffee. He was raving about what a big help you've been on the farm this year."

I tell Dad all about the basketball tryout. Mom tries to be interested, but she just doesn't get sports. Mostly she just gets mad watching me play the bench. Dad hardly made it to any games last year because he was having treatments for almost the whole season. It half-kills him to sit in the bleachers for a long time.

After supper, I'm dragging my butt upstairs to attack my fifty pounds of homework when Dad calls up to me. "A little one-on-one?"

I look down at him and shrug. Is he up for it? I don't really have time, but he hardly ever asks me to play anymore. "I've got an essay to write for English," I say. "But I can play for a bit."

"I think I can still take you." Dad punches me on the shoulder on the way by. "Just let me get changed." He comes back downstairs wearing an old Yankees sweatshirt, gray sweats that are hanging off him, and a winter hat. Seems like he's cold all the time now. The chemo did something to his blood, I think.

We play for a few minutes. He seems to get tired right away, so I take it pretty easy on him. His breathing's so noisy, I figure Mom'll come running out any minute now to see what's going on. Sounds like Jeff before he uses his puffer, or Darth Vader.

"Wow—Joe's really shown you a thing or two." He chucks me the ball, then collapses back into a lawn chair. "He was a take-charge kind of player back in our day. He could always see the whole floor, like he had eyes in the back of his head."

"I'm sorta like that, too." I sit down beside him. My record for spinning the ball on one finger is 62 seconds. "Hey, check this out. Coach says maybe I can play guard sometime this year." I drop the ball at 49, and it bounces off my toe. Rufus meows and scurries out of the way, just in time. "Only, I've gotta make the team first."

"He'd be crazy not to take you. You're due for a growth spurt, too. I grew six inches in Grade 8."

I wish. Mom says I've gotta be patient, that my body'll eventually catch up to my massive feet. My dad used to be six foot four. He's smaller now since the C Monster spread from his brain to his spine.

"I know I'm way better than last year, anyway."

"Gimme five!" Dad's grinning. He's like Hannah—they can always find something to be happy about.

We slap hands and get back up. Really, I get up and sort of pull Dad up out of his chair. Which isn't that hard since he's about forty pounds lighter than he used to be. He pats me on the shoulder. "Practice makes perfect. Thanks, little buddy."

We play SKUNK for a while. His shooting's still awesome. Some big universities were scouting Dad when he was in high school. He could've gotten a basketball scholarship, except he had to drop out and go to work when his dad died.

"That's all my head can handle," Dad says after our second game of SKUNK. He only gets to SKU and beats me both times. He gets these wicked dizzy headaches now if he tries to do too much. I hate cancer—even more than I hate Roy Williams.

"I'm just gonna stay out a few more minutes. Maybe I'll get some inspiration for my English essay on 'The Importance of Setting Goals.'"

I dribble the ball and watch him walk up the steps like an old man. He stops on every step and holds onto the railing with both hands. I get this real bad feeling deep down in my chest. My throat feels all tight and dry—like I'm gonna cry or something stupid like that. I turn around and drive in for a layup instead.

After he's gone inside, I sprint around the block a couple of times. I've got this crazy idea that I'm being chased by the ugly six-headed C Monster; I keep staring into the dark bushes, waiting for it to pop out, screeching at me like one of those banshees or mandrakes in *Harry Potter*. Nobody ever talks about it much, but I wonder how sick Dad really is—will he even get to see me play guard? It's hard to think about school when your brain's got that kind of major stuff going on ...

chapter six

Before I open my eyes the morning after the final tryout, I hear Hannah splashing around and singing in the bathtub. That rainbow song from *The Wizard of Oz.*

She says she's gonna be an actress or a singer or a dancer—maybe all three. She's forever dancing around the house and singing into a brush or a wooden spoon. She's not bad—for a little kid. Dad says she gets it from Mom, but I don't hear *her* singing around the house too much. She and Dad used to dance if a certain song came on the radio. Not so much now. I always hoped they'd never do it when Jeff and Andy were around. Really, I think it's kind of sick—I mean, they've been married, like, forever. Mostly everybody else's parents are split. Jeff is only around every other weekend; Andy spends half the summer on the other side of the country with his dad.

"I can give you a ride today—Dad's got a doctor's appointment. I'm going to drop him off on my way to work." When I get downstairs, Mom's brushing Hannah's hair and putting it into ponytails. Their hair's almost the same blonde color. King James, of course, has perfect wavy blond hair, no zits, Dad's tallness, and straight teeth. I got Dad's orange hair, freckles, and zits, and Mom's crooked teeth and puniness. Even better, if we have the money next year, I'm gonna become a metal mouth—for all of Grade 9 and 10. Can't wait for that pain. Two years without gummy worms—I'll probably starve to death.

"Sure." I gulp down some Cheerios. "I'm in serious trouble if I get another late slip. Plus Coach is posting the team list today."

"You'll make it—you almost made it last year, and you were only in Grade 7." Hannah stands on her tiptoes and reaches up to pat the top of my head. "Plus, you're way bigger this year."

Really, it seems like she's catching up to me. But I don't tell her that. Having a baby sister taller than you would be a blockbuster fail.

The list is short—only ten guys. I read the whole thing, top to bottom, bottom to top. What the ...! My face and ears start to burn. My heart does a vertical up into my throat somewhere. I rub my Adam's apple, press my lips together, blink, and go back to the top, read the list again, slower. It's like my mind's screaming out every name. The names of the top ten players at Oakdale Middle. Except for Bob Prescott.

"What's the matter, Blob?"

The smell of his aftershave makes me want to hurl. He shoves me out of the way and starts moving one fat finger back and forth under each name, with his lips moving, like I used to do when I first learned to read. I turn around and walk fast the other way. What happened? I aced that last tryout.

"Hey, Bobby. You going to the dance?" Maria's taping some balloons across the front of the stage when I speed-walk through the gym like I've got somewhere important to be.

"Nah, probably not ... maybe ... I ... I ..." I'm stuttering worse than usual. I want to go back and check the list one more time. Must be a mistake. Maybe my eyes were messed up from nerves.

"Bobby?"

I look at Maria and try to remember what she asked me.

"The dance. You going?" she repeats, waving an orange balloon in front of my face.

I mostly don't do dances because Mom's on the nightshift Fridays. Which means I've got to be home in case Dad or Hannah needs something, since James is always out somewhere being wonderful.

Before I can answer, Hannah skips up behind us. "You can go tonight, Bobby," she chirps, grabbing hold of my hand. "Remember? Mom's working the dayshift today." Another red flush starts at my neck and works its way up to the top of my head.

"Don't you have someplace to be?" I hiss at Hannah.

I yank my hand away and turn back to Maria. She's grinning and giving Hannah a thumbs-up.

"Oh, yeah—that's right ... guess I can go. Maybe Jeff and Andy will wanna go."

Hope she's not blown away by my enthusiasm. I'm not sure if I even do want to go, that's the thing. Mostly me and Jeff and Andy just hang around the canteen and the sound equipment when we do show up for dances. I don't even know if I *can* dance. It looks pretty easy, but I've never really tried. Well, except for Mom dancing me around the living room when I was little. A long time ago. The sound system's way more interesting than watching a bunch of kids shuffle around, even though that can be pretty funny sometimes.

"Fantastic! I'll see you there. Save me a dance," Maria says. "Gotta go."

"Can I see you for a minute, Bobby?"

I keep my eyes on his black sneakers and follow Coach into his office. "Have a seat," he says, staring at the floor. "You were the eleventh man." He folds his arms and sits one butt cheek on the edge of his desk. "It was a tough decision, but I needed more tall guys, and I've already got two experienced guards in Jordan and Roy. You've really improved, but keep working on your aggression."

I swallow hard and squint at his desk so my eyes don't tear up. "But I ... uh ... I thought I had good tryouts."

He goes around the desk, sits down in his chair, and nods. "You did. And if anybody gets injured, you're number one on my replacement list. I might even call you up to travel with us some. The rules allow for that."

I want to ask him if he knows what idiots Roy and Kyle are, but instead I thank him, head to class, and wish I was back in my Mr. Invisible days. The good thing is nobody cares much about basketball, so nobody asks if I made the team.

After school, I run home to get my chores done early. Why is it never James's turn to change Rufus's litter box?

"Guess I'm going to the dance tonight." I drop that into the conversation between bites of macaroni. "Where's Dad?"

"He's having a tray in his room—his meeting with Dr. Crosby didn't go so well." Mom keeps her eyes on her plate.

Then, like she remembers she's gotta be happy, she looks up and puts on a big sparkly smile. "The dance is a great idea. You should get out and have some fun. What are you going to wear?"

"I've got some stuff you can borrow," Hannah says. "Masks and makeup."

Wear? Crap, I never thought about that. I text Andy and Jeff. People in costumes get in for half-price, two bucks. Hannah lets me borrow her magician mask with the beard from last year, and I dig Dad's old purple and gold Oakdale jersey out of the back of my closet. Mom finds me a long curly black wig, a joke gift somebody gave Dad during his last round of chemo. Hannah braids it for me so I look like some kind of demented Wizard of Oz Dorothy.

Jeff and Andy look pretty stupid, too, when they pick me up. They're wearing surgical masks and those dew rag things that motorcycle guys and surgeons wear. Jeff's dad's a doctor. A face-lifter making a fortune off old people is how Jeff's mom describes him.

"Sucks about the team, eh?" I say.

Andy shrugs. "Didn't think I'd make it, anyway. You should've, though."

"Yeah," Jeff says. "You only suck half as much as us."

Andy yanks on one of my braids. "Who you supposed to be, anyway—Snoop Dogg?"

"Wazzup, Dawg?" I push my shoulders back and try to look gangsta. "I'm a bad muzzle dude, don't ya know? Fizzle, drizzle, guzzle, now, um ... Santa let it snow ..."

"Forget that shizzle." Andy checks me into a bush.

"Nice rapping, though," Jeff says, pulling me back out. "Bonus points for style."

"I need to watch more MuchMusic." I brush the twigs off Dad's jersey. "As if ..."

"Hey," Jeff says. "Maybe Sara will ask you to dance, Andy."

"As if." Andy went out with Sara Dennis in Grade 6. For three days. Until she told him he reminded her too much of the kids she babysat—that was a serious burn. I'm not sure girls are worth that kind of pain.

chapter seven

Besides the Grade 6 rookies, we're the only males that show up with any kind of costume. That's the story of my life. Mr. Invisible. Flying under the radar; following the rules when nobody else does.

"Hey, Blob—nice hair." Roy's got one arm around Franny Upton. He elbows me with his other arm, hard, and trips Jeff at the same time. Like Spiderman's mortal enemy, Dr. Octopus, minus the genius part. Why didn't he pick a contact sport like football or hockey instead of basketball? "Musta borrowed that jersey from a real basketball player, did ya?"

I don't say anything, just follow Jeff and Andy out to the hall. We yank off our masks and headgear, stuff them in my locker, then go back in the gym.

"Hey, Bobby!" Maria skips across the floor wearing big

green rubber boots. She's dressed like a scarecrow—a cute scarecrow. She's even got a stuffed crow pinned to one overall strap, with orange freckles painted all over her face and bits of straw sticking out everywhere. The freckles look way better on her than me.

"Hey, Maria ... cool costume." Why can't I ever think of something funny to say? The way my brain turns to straw soon as my lips move, it should be me wearing the scarecrow costume.

"Wanna dance?" She grabs my hand and starts pulling me out onto the floor.

"Um ... I guess so." I let her drag me out onto the gym floor while Jeff and Andy head to the canteen. Giant furry spiders, cobwebs, and glow-in-the-dark ghosts dangle from the basketball hoops. The stage is lit by a giant plastic pumpkin on top of the sound system. A volleyball net full of balloons hangs from the ceiling. "Nice decorations," I say.

"I know, right? Took us forever to blow up all those balloons," she says. "Even with an electric pump."

Lucky for me, the song's an old techno one where the beat doesn't change. Seems like my feet are doing the right thing, but I keep looking down at her big boots. It's like playing defense—just follow the other person's feet. It works out okay—at least Maria doesn't laugh at me or anything.

We line up at the fountain after the song. The gym's packed and super hot.

When somebody tries to prop the street doors open, the principal gets up on the stage to make an announcement. "The outside doors must remain closed—to keep out the riffraff." Looks to me like the riffraff already slithered in. Roy and Kyle are working their way through the crowd, jumping up to punch a spider here and there. Everybody's talking to them, laughing like they're stand-up comics. Why do people like them? Far as I can see, Roy's nasty to pretty much everybody, except maybe Kyle and Franny (a.k.a. Skanky).

She used to be a nice girl, way back in elementary. Kissed me once in Grade 6 when we were playing pool in her basement. Now she's got fingernails like lethal weapons, different colored hair every week, and she reeks of smoke half the time. She's always whispering in some other girl's ear, then cracking up while she looks around to see who's watching her.

Maria and I hang on the bench for a while, just watching people dance. It's almost as good as reality TV. When he's not making out with Franny in the corner, Roy's strutting around like some crazy rooster, with his chest sticking out and his pants hanging so low you can see his butt crack. Andy and Jeff must've ditched me—can't see them anywhere. Maria's got her shoulder pressed up against mine and our knees are touching. "You're a good dancer," I say, to keep from wondering what it would be like to kiss her.

She laughs. "In my dreams. I do take dance but it's ballet, not modern or hip hop." She kicks off her big boots and pushes them back under the bench, then wiggles her sock feet around in the air. "That's better—want to try again?"

It's a slow song. We find a spot on the crowded floor, she wraps her plaid arms around my neck, and we start spinning in circles, nice slow circles. She smells good, not like perfume, just clean, like laundry, or maybe like flowers, and she's humming. I rest my chin on top of her straw hat and close my eyes—until somebody slams into us. Roy. "Check that out," I whisper to Maria.

Roy's dancing with Franny, but apparently he doesn't notice it's a slow song, since he looks like he's having a seizure. Hard to believe he plays sports.

"This your little sister's friend?" When he notices us, he stops dancing and looks Maria up and down. His bottom lip's sticking out, like he's got his tongue stuffed behind it. He spits a nasty brown blob on the floor. Chewing tobacco? Roy chews tobacco? I thought only old men did that.

"You didn't see nothin', did ya?" he says. "Sorry I won't get to watch ya playing the D1 bench this year, Blob." Franny giggles like this annoying doll Hannah used to have.

"You and me both," I say.

"You know me." Maria pushes back the brim of her straw hat. "Maria MacLeod—your mom cooks at my dad's restaurant. We're in the same math class."

"Hey, right—didn't recognize you." He looks her up and down again. "Weren't so freckly last time I saw ya." Then he grabs Franny's hand and weaves off into the crowd.

"Do you think he's ...?"

"Oh, yeah ... hope Coach hears about that ... he'll be out for the year. Drinking at dances is at the top of his hate list. Maybe Roy'll puke in the can and get caught. Freakin' moron." I close my eyes again and try to forget about Roy, but the song's over.

"Want to sit down again?"

I follow Maria back to the bench. "The thing is, Roy doesn't have the greatest life," she says. "His mom has a little gambling problem. She practically lives in the VLT room at the tavern. He doesn't have a dad—at least, not one I ever heard about. My dad feels real sorry for Mrs. Williams."

"Me, too," I say, leaning back against the wall. "Having a kid like Roy."

"Dad's given her so many chances, but she's addicted. Her paycheck's spent before he even gives it to her. It's sad, really."

"That doesn't mean Roy needs to be such an idiot all the time. I mean, if he's got a bad life, that's okay. But he's just plain old mean, and by mean, I mean he's freakin' evil!" I cram my fists into my pockets. "Hey! Maybe if he gets caught, I can get his spot on the D1 team."

"You didn't make it?"

I shake my head. "Nope. Coach said I was the last person cut. Said he might bring me up from D2 if somebody gets injured."

"That would be good. And maybe you'll get to play more on the other team." Marie jumps up and claps her hands. "Let's dance again—me and my mom love Elton John! And 'Rocket Man's' one of my favorites. I'm learning to play it on my guitar."

"Cool song name," I say, putting my arms around her waist.

Nine-thirty comes super fast. When they drop the balloons, Maria kisses me on the cheek. It's so fast, I'm not even sure it really happened. But Jeff and Andy make fun of me all the way home.

"Smoochy, smoochy, lover-boy," Jeff says, while Andy wiggles down the street ahead of us making kissing noises in the air.

I give them both a shove, but I'm smiling. I know they think Maria's all right—for a girl.

When I get home, I try to pick out "Rocket Man" on my guitar, then lie in bed for a while, staring out the window at the stars and thinking about the dance. Maybe Grade 8 won't be so bad after all ...

At least there's one girl that doesn't think I'm a total loser.

And on the D2 team, I won't have to spend so much time being a duster. Collecting dust on the end of the bench.

chapter eight

"*Somewhere, over the rainbow ...*"

I am *so* starting to hate that song—especially first thing on a Saturday morning. Hannah wants to be Dorothy in the Grade 5 play this year, so she's learning all *The Wizard of Oz* songs. I think she'd make a better Munchkin, but I don't tell her that.

It's Saturday, though, my day to play with the little kids in the Pee Wee program, so it's all good. I take a nice long hot shower and think about dancing with Maria last night. Wonder if I'll see her this weekend.

"Ow!" I bang on the sides of the shower.

"Sorry," Mom calls upstairs. "Just brushing my teeth." The pipes in our old house are all messed up, so only one person at a time can run water.

When I get home from helping out with the Pee Wees,

Mom's cooking pancakes for brunch. Her pancakes are the best—the big fluffy but chewy kind. And she makes her own wild blueberry syrup. I eat six and I'm stuffed, but there's still one left in the pan.

"Flip you for it," I say. "Oooh, sweet pun—get it?"

Mom rolls her eyes. "I get it—I am, after all, the head pancake flipper around here."

When I'm done, she pushes up her sleeves and starts doing the dishes. Hannah's at the rink for figure skating. Dad and James are still in bed. "Feel free to dry," she says. "Dishtowels are in the middle drawer, in case you've forgotten."

What's up with that? She never asks me to do the dishes.

"So, we should talk about Dad's appointment yesterday." Mom runs some more hot water. The sink's already pretty full; the bubbles are up to her elbows.

"Ooo ... kay." It's the kind of thing where I like to know what's going on, but I don't—if you know what I mean. It's mostly nothing but bad news with the C Monster.

"Dr. Crosby says he's worried it's spread ... again." She stops, stares out the window, and wipes her drippy nose on her sleeve. "Into his lungs this time. That's why he gets tired so easily and has trouble ..." she closes her eyes and puts one soapy hand over her mouth to hide her jiggly lips "... breathing."

"Oh." I dry the same plate about fifty times, until I feel dizzy. My heart's pounding in my ears, trying to block out her words. It's hard to think, like somebody pushed the Pause button in my brain—nothing but static.

She goes back to washing. "He thinks more radiation might help. Dad's not sure he can take any more treatment. It makes him so sick."

"That sucks," I say with my usual gift for words. "Big time."

"We need to understand that there is no cure for this. The best we can hope for is a little more time. It's not good ... I'm sorry, Bobby."

Random. Like it's her fault or something ...

This is so awkward. I almost feel like I have to hug her. The last time I did was in Grade 4 when Gram died. "Does Hannah know?" I ask instead, tucking my hands in under my armpits.

"I've just told her that Dad's really sick, but she knows about the C Monster, and I know she sees how weak he is." Mom blasts some more hot water into the sink. "We all need to help keep him comfortable. I'm going to take some time off work."

'Nuff said. That's *so* not what I want to hear. I know what taking time off work means—Mr. Baldwin, our gym teacher, did that last year. His wife ended up dying two months later.

Sometimes, I'm scared to look at Dad. Scared I'll see the tumor bulging right out of his head or something, like in some horror movie. Like some mutant prickly sea urchin scratching up his brain. "That sucks ... totally." I finish drying the plates and stack them in the cupboard.

Mom looks up at me and tries to smile. "What are you up to today? And are you remembering to wear your glasses?"

I ignore that last part and nod. "I'm gonna bike out to Joe's this afternoon. He said he's got lots of jobs for me, and he'll help me work on my ball handling."

"It'll do you good to get out of the house," she says, pulling the plug. "Looks like it's going to be a pretty quiet day around here, and it's a beautiful day for a bike ride."

Dad and James and me used to bike out on the dykes. We'd go for miles. I was in the middle then, too, but it was a sweet place to be, in between my two heroes. Being a kid was way more fun then.

I ride my bike hard—I can't stop thinking about Dad. It's so not fair. He's a good guy, for a parent. Why couldn't the C Monster have picked on some child abuser? Or maybe a mass murderer? How about a suicide bomber?

I try to chill and act normal, but Joe sees right away there's something wrong. "Want to talk about it?" We clean out the horse stalls and I tell him what Mom said. He doesn't ask about the team, so I don't tell him. I don't want to have a total meltdown.

"I remember your dad being in almost the same boat, Bobby, when we were in Grade 12. Only worse. His whole life changed the day his dad dropped dead of a heart attack." Joe hands me the pitchfork. "Just pile up some clean straw in each stall ... not too much."

"Like this?" I say, stabbing a forkful. "Out of the way, Bailey."

Bailey drops her tail between her legs and runs to hide behind the tractor.

Joe nods. "It was tough for Rob, having to quit school and take a job at the grocery store to help his mom. He had two little brothers to think about."

"Yeah ..." What will we do for money if Dad ... well, if Dad doesn't get better? He's ... well, he used to be ... a bank manager. A real smart guy with numbers.

"But, hey ... there are always miracles. You hear about them every day. We can't give up hope. Not yet." Joe punches me on the shoulder, his version of a guy hug.

Work makes the time go by fast. We're building a chicken coop inside the barn; pounding nails gives me something else to think about.

After a while, Joe says, "Hungry? I'll see if I can rustle us up a snack."

The chickens are running around free, clucking and bobbing their crazy heads up and down. The strutting rooster reminds me of Roy. Being pissed at him makes me bang my thumb, and I start to laugh. I get laughing so hard that I start crying. All of a sudden, I don't know what's going on. I'm sitting on the floor, curled up in a ball, sucking on my thumb, and bawling like a baby. Bailey sits down beside me and starts licking my face. I use one of her warm floppy ears to sop up my tears.

When Joe comes back with hot chocolate and crackers, he doesn't say anything, just pulls me up off the floor and sits me down on a bale of hay. He puts on some Johnny Cash, gets me an old horse blanket and a pillow, and lets me cry. I feel like I'm losing it, like I'm stuck on the Tilt-a-Whirl and everything's spinning. Joe keeps working, whistling along with the music. Acting like everything's normal. I wish.

When I'm done sniffling, he stops hammering and says, "If you're feeling better, we could play some one-on-one.

It's been a while."

I take a mouthful of cold hot chocolate, fold up the blanket, then get up off the hay bale. "Didn't make D1—again." I kick at some loose straw on the floor. "Coach did say I might get some floor time if somebody gets injured."

Joe shakes his head. "Rough week, then. I thought for sure you'd make it this year. All the more reason to work harder on your skills. Let's go, kiddo. I think I can take you." He sweeps up the hay so we can see the lines he painted on the floor, and I get the ball out of the old feed bin where he keeps it. He made the rim himself out of some old copper pipe.

We play for a few minutes but I can't get into it. "I suck even worse than usual. Probably I should just go home," I say finally. "Can't get my head in the game."

"Remember ... Michael Jordan didn't make his junior high team ... and look where he ended up."

"Right."

Joe gives me an extra twenty bucks in my pay envelope. "Treat your family to one of Valentino's pizzas. With the works. Double cheese."

"Thanks, Joe—for everything," I mumble. "Sorry about ... you know ..."

"My door's always open for you, Bobby." He gives me a real guy hug, with one arm. "Your dad's a tough guy. He'll be okay. You'll see."

"I wish."

I bike home slowly. Until I see some kids out trick-or-treating, I forget it's Halloween. Lucky them. Mom wouldn't let me go out this year after some old people got pissy at us for being too big last year.

When I get back to town, I bike past a couple of tall Grim Reapers cutting across the school parking lot. "Hey, Blob ... nice costume!" I want to ask Roy where he got the sweet Pokémon pillowcase, but I don't bother. When I get to our street, the sun's just setting and the sky's all full of streaky red and purple and gold clouds. I see one tiny star and think of Hannah and how I wasn't there to see her Dorothy costume. She always makes a wish on the first star she sees. What the heck—it can't hurt. Nobody will ever know.

Star light, star bright, first star I see tonight.

Wish I may, wish I might, have the wish I wish tonight ...

I don't need to tell you what I wished for ...

chapter nine

Dad's reading the paper Sunday morning when I drag myself downstairs. His hair's wet and it looks like he shaved. Most days, he looks all gray—his whiskers, his hair, and his skin—like an old man. An old man living on the streets. He used to tickle us like crazy with his weekend whiskers when we were little.

I'm not that hungry because I've got the game-gut feeling, all scared and nervous. Like my gut's full of wiggling baby snakes. I'm kind of scared to look at Dad, but I peek sideways out the corner of my eye as I'm pouring my milk. He stayed in bed all day yesterday; I expected he'd look sicker today, now that the C Monster's on the move again. I didn't even get a chance to tell him yet about not making the team.

"Thought we might head up to the cottage for the

day." He sets his cereal bowl down on the floor for Rufus to lick.

I whip around and look right at him, splash a little milk on the counter. "Really? We haven't been there in, like, forever." I try to sound excited ... only Maria just texted me about hanging out in the park this afternoon.

"Lots to do up there before winter," Dad says. "The dock and the raft, draining the pipes—that kind of thing."

"We could do that," I say. "Maybe Joe can come. One last swim for Bailey."

"Hmmm—maybe I'll give him a call," he says. But he doesn't look happy about it. It kills Dad that he can't do all the work he used to. Was that a pun? But I know Mom and I can't do it all alone, and James almost never comes to the lake with us anymore.

The thing about cancer is you can almost believe it's not there sometimes. Like when you wake up from a bad dream—you're so stoked it wasn't real that you feel all giddy. Today almost feels like any other Sunday—so far. But something always happens to mess things up, make you remember the C Monster's not just a nightmare.

Mom and Hannah make some sandwiches and pack the cooler. "What kinda chocolate bar do you want, Bobby?" Hannah asks, holding her bulgy pillowcase open. "I've got tons. And I'll share, even though you missed seeing me in my Dorothy costume."

I shrug. "I like 'em all, except the coconut ones."

"Mr. Big for me," James says, coming into the kitchen flexing his biceps.

"Are you kidding—you're coming?" James hardly ever comes to the lake with us in the summer because he works at a kids' camp over in Millwood.

He pours himself a big glass of OJ, chugs it, then muffles a burp with his hand. "Wouldn't miss it."

"The leaves are peaking, don't you think, Rob?" Mom asks as she drives us up into the mountains. In our BC life—Before Cancer—Dad always drove. Now, the insurance company says he can't because of his dizziness.

"I'd say another week or two," he answers. "We haven't had too many frosty nights yet."

They have the exact same conversation every fall. This could be a regular Sunday trip to the cottage. But it isn't ... not really. It's like there's a big black invisible monster in the car with us, taking up a ton of space. We're all trying our best to pretend it's not there. Like the kid in your class with no friends, B.O., and greasy hair.

The cottage looks deserted when we get there, like it's already closed up for the winter. There's a big broken pine tree stretched out across the front lawn. Just missed the deck. We haven't cut the grass since August. Inside, there's lots of dead flies all around the windows. It smells cold and musty.

"No point in opening all the windows." Mom sighs and sweeps some of the flies onto the floor with her glove. "We won't be here long enough."

Hannah picks up an oven mitt and shakes it. "Ewww ..." A bunch of stuffing and tiny black turds fall on the counter.

"For such cute little things, mice are sooo ... disgusting."

As soon as Joe comes, we get to work. Bailey chases the squirrels for a while, then splashes right into the lake, even though there are already icy spots along the edges. "She's looking a little pudgy," Joe says. "Do her good to get some extra exercise."

James, Joe, and me work together, taking the dock apart, lifting it out and using the pedal boat to tow the diving raft to shore. Joe makes a big deal about Dad being the supervisor, huddled in his Adirondack chair, wrapped up in a sleeping bag, while we splash around, shivering in the freezing water. Even with hip waders, my feet are icebergs when we're done. Hannah gathers some branches and Mom starts a fire on the beach to warm us up.

"Think I'll just go in for a little nap." Dad yawns and stretches. "No place like the lake for sleeping. I'll help you cut up that tree when I'm all rested up."

After he goes in, we drag the big tree away from the cottage out onto the lane. Joe cuts it up with his chainsaw and James and me stack it next to the shed. "Should be nice and dry by next summer," Joe says. Yeah, right—next summer. Scares the crap out of me thinking about it ...

We rake leaves and throw them on the fire. Hannah makes a wreath out of some pine branches, acorns and pinecones, red and yellow leaves. I watch Mom filling the bird feeders and think of Maria and her birdseed bread. Wonder if she's at the park today. Even though I know there's no service, I check my phone. Wish we had Internet at the lake. We don't even have TV.

I try to look chill when James asks me if I want to take the canoe out after lunch. Since he started high school, we never do anything together anymore.

"It's been a while, eh?"

"Uh-huh." I automatically get in the bow and he takes the stern. It used to be Dad in the back, steering, James in the front, and me in the middle.

"That really sucks about Dad, huh?" he says. "And the D1 team. Change sides."

"Totally." I switch my paddle to the left and try to match my strokes to his. "Wish we could do something."

"About Dad or the team?"

"Both," I say. "I wish."

"We already do the grass and our other chores. But I know what you mean. There's gotta be something else we can do—just for Dad. We should shoot some hoop together, too. You and me."

"Hmmm ..." I stare straight ahead and wonder when he'd find the time to squeeze me into his busy schedule of important stuff. I'm trying to look for the giant turtle we saw in the summer, but the lake's almost putting me to sleep it's so calm. Watching the canoe split the water kind of hypnotizes you, like watching a fire.

"I'm doing my major Biology project on brain tumors— how they affect people's short-term memory," James says. "Change sides. I'm thinking I might try for med school. Be a cancer doctor someday. An oncologist."

I turn around and grin at him. "Really? That'd be seriously

sweet. Did you tell Dad?"

"Not yet. I'm still thinking about it. Trying to get my head around another ten years of school."

"Wish we had tons of money to give to the onco-whatevers, so they could figure out how to kill the freakin' C Monster." I lay my paddle across the canoe and we drift for a bit. "If there was just a pill you could take—y'know, like for ear infections."

James flicks water at the back of my head with his paddle. "There are lots of drugs that help, but cancer's a little different from an ear infection."

"Duh!" I splash him back. We paddle hard for a couple of minutes. My brain's working overtime, all clear and precise like the reflection of the trees in the lake. Must be the fresh air. "Hey, you know how they're always having hockey games to raise money for stuff? We could organize a basketball game, a fundraiser game for cancer research. Like the Terry Fox Run we do at school every year."

"Maybe. But who'd pay to watch us? They can watch for free any other time, and we still only get a few dozen people out."

"Yeah." We drift some more out toward the little islands in the middle of the lake. "I guess you're right." I think I hear the old turtle snapping, but it's just a woodpecker looking for lunch on Geezer's Island. There used to be an old guy, a hermit, living in a shack on it when we first got the cottage. He must've died. We haven't seen him in forever. Geezers ... hmmm ...

I start paddling again, then twist around. "What about an

old-timers' game? The old guys who used to play at Oakdale could take on your team."

He presses his lips together and shakes his head. "I dunno. The hockey team did that one time. Only raised enough money to buy new sticks." James pokes me in the shoulder with the grip of his paddle. "Plus it sounds like a *whole* lot of work. Change sides. If we did, though, you'd have to play, too ... now you're not a Stick-boy anymore."

"Maybe ..." I'd really be Mr. Invisible with all those high school giants. "I'll see. If I'm not good enough for D1 at the middle school, I could never play with you guys."

He pokes me again with his paddle. "Sure you could. You just need to be more aggressive. Own the floor. Think positive."

"Coach says the same thing. That I'm not hungry enough for the ball."

"Did that derp Roy Williams make it?"

"Duh. He's at least six inches taller than me. The fact he's an idiot doesn't matter when it comes to ball."

"I used to be scared to touch the ball, back when I first started playing in middle school," James says. "I was pretty small then."

"Seriously?"

"Yeah—but Coach told me to think about my legs exploding up the floor when I got the ball. I used to think of them like rockets, pretend I was some kind of superhero flying up the floor."

Picturing King James pretending to be a superhero makes me laugh. Wind sprints and line drills are always the best parts of practice for me. No random elbows and hip checks to worry about then. Especially if you're out front of everybody.

"You're fast, too. Think about your legs like two skinny rockets next time you're out there. You'll burn up the floor, leave everybody in your smoke. What was the name of that superhero you used to pretend to be?"

"Mr. Invisible," I mumble. "When I was, like, six."

"You've gotta be the opposite of Mr. Invisible on the court," he says. "Seriously, let's go out on the driveway after supper tonight. Maybe I can show you a few tricks."

We paddle back to shore, talking all the way.

"Ssssh!" We drift for a bit and watch a blue heron fishing in a swampy area. When he spots us, he spreads his massive wings and takes off, disappearing above the trees.

"Hey, what about Hank Jones?" I say. "The Birdman." Hank's the only guy from around here to make it to the NBA. He got his nickname because he was so fast it looked like he was flying up the floor. Only played two years before he blew out his knee. Now he talks basketball on TV.

"It'd be wicked to have somebody famous play for the Geezers," James says. "Now him, people *would* pay to see."

We decide to keep our idea a secret for a while. It might not work out; we're gonna need *a lot* of help. "I'm crazy busy with school and basketball," James says while we're hanging the canoe up in the shed. "But I'll do what I can. You're a good organizer, and your buddies will probably help out."

"Help out with what? Can I help?" Hannah's hanging

her wreath on the front door. "So the squirrels won't get hungry."

"Never mind with what," I say, pulling her hat down over her eyes.

"And you don't need to worry about the squirrels," James says. "They'll be packing their bags, moving inside, and rooting through the cupboards the minute they see us disappearing down the lane."

After the van's all packed, Dad finally comes out and walks around the cottage, real slow. He stands for a long time just looking out at the lake, with his hands in his pockets. It is nice—the orange and yellow trees and their identical twins in the blue water. It's so quiet my ears are ringing. "My little piece of heaven," Dad says. He says that every year on the last day, but this year's different.

We all watch Dad watching the lake. His baggy red cottage sweater looks way too big for him. Nobody says anything for the longest time. Is he wondering if he'll ever see the lake again? Even Bailey stays quiet for a couple of minutes. Then she jumps out of the truck, chases a squirrel across the grass, and splashes into the water for one last swim. She comes out and shakes all over Joe, then we all laugh, say goodbye to them, and climb into the van.

"Bye Cottage! Bye Lake! Merry Christmas! Happy New Year. See you in the spring!" Hannah keeps waving out the back window all the way down the lane.

Nobody else says anything. Dad keeps staring out the window until the cottage disappears from sight.

chapter ten

"*Mmmooooo!*" Hannah gave me this crazy cow alarm clock for my birthday. It was kind of funny—the first time. Now it just bugs me, and it ticks like a bomb. I only set the alarm when I absolutely have to.

Like last night. I need to get to school early today, get in some gym time before the D1 season-opener this afternoon—against Millwood, just in case somebody gets injured and Coach calls me in. He's been letting me practice with the D1 team to give me some extra court time. Millwood beat us in the big Snowball tournament *and* the playoffs last year. In fact, Millwood beats our school at pretty much every sport, even ping-pong. I don't know what they eat out there, but their short guy is five foot nine. Probably all on steroids.

"Hey." Maria leans one shoulder against my locker. "I didn't see you in the park the other day." Turquoise ribbons. Which means she was looking for me ...

"Yeah ... we went to the cottage ... closed it up for the winter. You guys play tennis?"

"For a bit ... then we kicked a soccer ball around. We didn't have enough people for a real game."

We walk to class together. The snakes are partying in my gut all day. Hope not too many kids hang around to watch. I want to play guard, but I don't—if you know what I mean. Not that I'll probably get called in anyway.

"You coming to the game?" I ask Maria at lunchtime. "Me and Andy are doing the scoreboard and the clock—exciting stuff."

"I hope so," she says. "I ..."

Just then Roy comes up behind Andy and slams his fat fist down on my yogurt tube. BAM! SPLAT! Maria's face and hair are covered in sticky blueberry yogurt. Just like in the cartoons, except not that funny ... only everybody around us is laughing.

Maria stands up sputtering and wipes her face with her lunch bag. "What the ... what do you think you're ..."

But Roy's gone. He does that stuff all the time, like it's his job to make other people feel like crap. Nobody ever rats him out because we all know how evil he is—the Payback King.

Maria stomps off to the bathroom. Andy, Jeff, and me try to act like nothing happened and keep eating.

"I'm going to the office," Maria says when she comes

back. Her hair's dripping wet and her cheeks are bright pink. "It just sucks that he gets away with stuff like that!"

"What she said," Jeff says, grinning through a mouthful of cheeseburger.

"He's a wanksta. Remember what happened to Andy?" I remind her.

Andy ditched Roy as his lab partner after Roy spilled vinegar and baking soda on Andy's fifty-dollar calculator just to see what would happen. Next day, Andy's locker was all beat up, like somebody took a hammer and screwdriver to it, so he complained to the office. Next morning, the whole thing was kicked in, and all his stuff was spread over the hall. Roy must've hidden and done it after the janitors left.

"You're probably right, but still ..." Maria pounds her fists on the table. Or, at least, she tries to. But her fists are pretty tiny. "It's just *so* not fair."

Only about twenty people are in the bleachers after school. Maria's in the top row with Hannah. Last year, Hannah was in a cheerleader phase. Used to show up at my games with pom-poms and everything. So embarrassing.

Roy's the starting point guard. He's a ball hog, but he sets up a few nice plays and scores some baskets—two three-pointers. Then, just before halftime, he does a Dr. Octopus, tries to trip a Millwood player on a breakaway, and ends up going down himself. He gives the other guy a cobra stare, pushes himself up slowly, and limps over to the bench. Coach calls a time-out, gets an ice pack out for Roy's ankle, then tells him to take off his jersey.

The gut snakes start squirming when Coach looks over at the table and gives me the wave. I point to myself and stand up. He nods.

"I've got this," Andy says. He pats the control box and gives me a high-five, and I run over to the bench.

"How fast can you get dressed?" Coach throws me Roy's jersey.

"Two seconds." I've already got my sneakers on and shorts under my sweats.

"Think you can play backup guard?" Coach says. "Just for a few minutes. Jordan's got a migraine, and I want to use Luke under the basket."

"I hope so," I say. Except I still don't have my glasses.

"Remember—keep your head up and think aggressive. Use your speed. You need to own the whole floor. Can't be invisible when you're playing guard."

I stare at him. How did he know about Mr. Invisible?

"Don't screw this up for us, Blob!" Roy hisses in my ear before we break.

"Good to know you've got my back," I hiss back.

The half goes pretty good for us. Joe and my dad show up a few minutes after it starts. Dad's using his cane, but he manages to make it up into the second row. I make all four of my foul shots and only lose the ball once my whole shift, so I'm happy.

Second shift, I send a bad baseball pass to Kyle. It goes off his fingertips and hits the back wall. Great. He runs up to me, right in front of the Millwood bench, and gives me a hard shoulder. Then helps me up so it looks like an accident.

"Nice move, Blob—Roy said you're too stupid to play guard. D'ya need new glasses, ya tool?" Then Kyle turns around and aims a big noisy slart right at me. A slippery fart that makes all the Millwood players burst out laughing. The ref doesn't notice; he's busy wiping sweat off the key.

Coach calls for a time-out, even though we just had one.

"Kyle—you're outta there!" He jerks his thumb at the bench. "Join your buddy on the bench. Maybe the two of you can figure out why there's no 'I' in TEAM. One team, one goal, no egos." He looks over at me. "Nice work out there, Bob."

I work some sweet plays after that. Every time I get the ball, I think of James and the rockets. The guys on the bench—well ... except Roy and Kyle—do lots of cheering. I choke on my last foul shot and we lose the game, but only by three.

Roy limps up to me outside the locker room. "Sweet job, Blob—we would've won if I was guard. And, hey—what's wrong with your old man? He looks half-dead."

Andy and Jeff look like they're ready to pound Roy. Me, too. Instead, I pick up my bag and say, "Maybe he is, you idiot," and walk out. I actually say it loud enough for him to hear. I am not gonna let that derp ruin my season—or my life.

Jeff and I spend an hour in the driveway before supper one night. I finally got my glasses back so I'm kicking his butt. In between plays, I tell him about the Geezers game. "So I was thinking, you, me, and Andy can set up a Web site for people to get information, find out how to donate, where to get tickets and stuff."

"Whoa!" he says, after I shoulder him off the ball for the third time. "Okay, I'll help you. But what's up with the violence?"

"My bad. James told me to think of the guy on me as my worst enemy," I say. "I was acting like you were Roy."

I meet Maria at the library after supper. After I help her figure out the surface area of a rectangular prism, I tell her about the Geezers game. "And since you're so organized and all that, do you want to be our publicity and marketing person? You know tons of people, don't you? And didn't you get first place in the Art Fair?"

The whole time I'm talking, she's got this big pumpkin grin on her face. It's like her whole body's grinning.

"Yeah, for that spooky Mona Lisa painting of my grandma—somehow I did her eyes so it looks like she's watching you no matter where you move. I'd love to help!" She gives my arm a hug.

Miss Gladwin shoots us a sour look from behind the desk, where she's perched like some kind of hawk. Waiting to swoop down on noisy kids.

"That is such an awesome idea!" Maria whispers, bouncing up and down in her chair. "When can I start?"

"Now, I guess. We're hoping to do it over the Christmas holidays." I try to act cool, pretend I'm not blushing. She gets out some paper and we brainstorm. Well, mostly she brainstorms and I listen.

"My dad buys lots of advertising for his restaurant—newspapers, radio, even cable TV. I bet he could get them to give us some advertising time or space. Plus my Uncle Jack does a lot of desk-top publishing. I know he'll help me come up with a great poster. Especially since it's to help raise money for cancer research. We can probably print them in the tech lab at school."

She's thinking and talking so fast my ears can hardly keep up. It's way more fun working on this with her than James. Since his season started, seems he never has time for Mr. Invisible, either to shoot some hoop or help with the game.

"*Shhhhh!*" Miss Gladwin glares at us from behind the desk.

I walk home with Maria and jog the rest of the way to my street. Crispy brown leaves are blowing everywhere in the gusty wind. Feels like a storm's coming. It's really dark at my house. No lights ... just the solar butterflies in the garden. A burst of adrenalin makes me sprint the last block. The van's gone. The back door's unlocked. In fact, it's wide open.

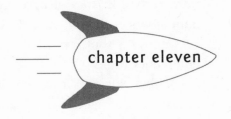

chapter eleven

I don't even yell to see if anybody's home. I shoo Rufus away from my ankles, then read the messy note scribbled on an envelope on the kitchen table.

Took Dad to hospital. I'll call when I can. Don't worry,
Love, Mom xoxo

"Don't worry!" I say out loud. "What's that supposed to mean?" I crush the note and chuck it at the wall. Rufus jumps down off his chair and runs to hide behind the garbage can. How will I get to the hospital? It's at least five miles from our house. I turn on the lights to help me think. *Crunch!* I pick a sticky red piece of glass out of the bottom of my sneaker.

I run back outside and get my bike out of the shed. Lucky

for me, I bought a geeky headlight in the summer for my rides home from the farm. I ride hard. It's like the wind's trying to push me backwards, box me out so I can't get to where I need to be. After about fifteen minutes, the freezing rain starts. I'm soaked and my hands are frozen to the handlebars by the time I finally get to the hospital.

"Hanny!" I spot her walking down the hall outside the emergency room.

"Bobby!" She runs up to me, throws her arms around me, and shoves her face into my jacket. "Brrr ... you're all cold and wet."

"What's going on?" I ask, backing away.

"It was so scary. He fell down when Mom was at the store. I was upstairs and there was this big crash. I think he was getting a drink. There was tomato juice all over the floor and broken glass."

I almost smile. "That's what that sticky stuff was. Did he get knocked out?"

"Maybe just for a second. I think he bumped his head pretty hard, and he puked when he stood up. I picked up all the glass, though, and Rufus ate most of the throw-up."

"Good job, Hannah." I pat her on the shoulder and she hugs me again.

When Dad first started getting dizzy, we were at the mall this one time when he fell. Some nosy old lady comes up to me and asks if Dad was drunk. He's flaked out in a puddle of coffee, half knocked out, and she wants to call the police. Some people just need to get a life.

We sit down on the blue vinyl couch in the waiting room.

Hannah leans into me while I flip through some women's magazines and try to chill. Recipes, clothes, and makeovers.

"How to Look Twenty When You're Really Forty."

"What's Your Decorating Personality?"

"A Dozen Festive Party Drinks."

We both look at the clock a million times. It must be broken. I keep seeing Dad falling and the C Monster exploding like a bomb inside his head.

"I hate hospitals." Hannah yawns and buries her nose in my sleeve. "They smell bad. Like bathroom cleaner."

Just after nine, Mom comes out through the emergency room doors. She's as white as the walls and looks totally wiped. And when did she get so skinny?

"It's okay." Her smile's like a scribbly red line. "He's got a pretty green shiner and a big goose egg, but he's okay." We stand up and she gives us both a hug. "Let's go home."

"Can't we see him?" I ask.

"He's asleep already. Maybe tomorrow."

"You mean he's not coming home with us?" Hannah asks.

Mom shakes her head. "They're keeping him overnight, to be on the safe side. We'll most likely pick him up tomorrow."

We load my bike into the van and head home. The freezing rain's already melted, and the sky's clear and full of stars. I hear Hannah wishing to herself in the backseat; she's mumbling so I can't tell what she's wishing for, but I can imagine. The house is too dark and quiet when we get there. James is away at a tournament. I tried to text him, but he must've turned off his phone. Not like there's anything he could do anyway.

"Brrrrr!" Mom takes off her jacket and shivers. "I think it's time for our first fire. Let me get some wood."

"I'll do it." I jump up. It'll give me something to keep me busy.

After I get the fire going, the three of us sit around the woodstove. Hannah makes us hot chocolate, which is more like hot marshmallows with a bit of chocolate.

"I wish Dad and James were here." She yawns and snuggles up to Mom on the couch.

"Dad does love the first fire of the year," Mom says, stroking her hair.

"Remember how he says we're like Goldilocks and the four bears, hibernating for winter?"

I snort. "Isn't it past your bedtime?" That's how I'm supposed to act; the big brother and all that, since James isn't here. But really, I love that stupid idea; the idea of our whole family chillaxin', warm and safe for the long winter. I stare into the fire and let it hypnotize me into not thinking. I grunt when Mom gets up to take Hannah to bed. A few minutes later, I make sure the doors are locked, then follow them. All of a sudden, I feel like I just played back-to-back ball games.

I fall into bed, but I can't sleep. It's cold upstairs. I pull the blankets up over my head and shuffle my feet back and forth on the sheet to warm them up. I can't stop thinking about Dad, all by himself in that stinking hospital room. I got a concussion once, from soccer. They woke me up every hour to check my eyes and make sure my brain was okay. Hope Dad gets some sleep. And that Papa Bear comes home tomorrow ... can you believe I just thought that? Good thing nobody can see inside my brain ...

chapter twelve

Intense news when I get to school in the morning. Roy and Kyle got picked up by the cops for jumping three little kids out trick-or-treating last week. They hid behind some bushes on a dark path, jumped out screaming, took all the kids' candy, and scared the crap out of them. How freakin' evil is that? All for a few puny chocolate bars?

The talk is Roy'll be going on a holiday—to Waterton, the youth detention center. So far, he's still at school doing his rooster strut in the halls. Looking proud of himself, like being a criminal's so cool. Maybe he finally went too far. One of the kids is on my Pee Wee team; Brian's only five. Maria babysits him, and she says he hasn't been able to sleep since then because of the monster dreams. He's even scared to walk to school.

At lunchtime, Roy and Kyle have their cafeteria table

all to themselves. Usually they've got about ten other Roy wannabes hanging around. Roy's not looking quite so rooster when they leave, but he manages to fire a slitty-eyed stare at us on his way past.

D1 and D2 share the gym for practice after school, but the criminals don't show up. Coach calls us all in to tell us Roy and Kyle are off the D1 team until the case goes to court.

"The police have three witnesses willing to testify that they saw Roy and Kyle that night, walking around carrying a couple of kids' cartoon pillowcases," Coach says. "Roy was wearing a Grim Reaper hood, but he's the only one in town with shiny red basketball shoes."

Hope he doesn't think one of the rats was me. I've got enough other stuff going on.

"And two of the witnesses recognized Kyle's voice. But, of course, the law says they're innocent until proven guilty." Coach looks at me. "If it's okay with you, Bobby, I'd like to move you up. At least until Roy and Kyle get straightened away. You, too, Jeff."

"Seriously?"

He nods.

"No problem." I grin and give Jeff a shoulder. "I've been working on being pushier."

Coach stands up and blows his whistle. "Let's see what you've got. Come on in, everybody. Let's play ball!"

I do the rocket legs thing every time I get a breakaway. Coach even calls me on an offensive foul one time. But he's grinning after he blows the whistle.

"Looking good, Prescott," he says when practice is done. "I like what I'm seeing!"

Maria's standing by the gym door. Is she waiting for me? Red ribbons today—and looks like she's holding something behind her back.

"I've been working on the poster." She holds it up. "How do you like it so far?"

She used a giant black and white yearbook photo of my dad's 1982 high school team with their ridiculously short shorts. Somehow she made them all into funny old geezers with canes and gray hair and all. Then she took a picture of this year's team and gave them all NBA players' bodies— they look sweet. James is about 6'10" in the picture. Looks like Shaq's body. HOOP HEROES 4 HEALTH is in big purple letters across the top, and between the two pictures, she kind of stole a book title. *That Was Then … This is Now—Who's #1?*

"Sweet!" I pass it back to her and we start walking home.

"I can still Photoshop you into the Rookie picture, if you want me to."

"I dunno … I'm thinking about it … James's coach said I could play, but I might just run the canteen or something. Or maybe I'll take tickets."

"Hannah and her friends already asked to do that," she says, pushing into me with her shoulder. "Sorry …"

"Maybe the scoreboard, then." I point to Joe in the poster picture. "That's my dad's friend, Joe, the guy whose farm I work at. He said he'll play on the Geezers team, although he didn't love the idea of being called a geezer." Joe said he wasn't over the hill yet when I asked him. And that he wished Dad could play, too. Him and me both.

When we get to her corner, Maria puts one hand on my jacket sleeve and says, "See you tomorrow?"

I give her a thumbs-up, then jog off to pick up Hannah from her friend's house.

She's waiting for me outside. "We need to hurry, Bobby—did you forget about Dad?" I grab her hand and we take off running.

Mom's humming and cooking dinner when we get there. Her humming's sort of like the thermometer for our family. Or maybe a barometer. The louder she hums, the better things are.

"Mmmmm ..." I sniff loudly. "Ham?" Since she's been off work, the food's been a lot tastier.

She opens the oven door and plunks the roaster down on the counter. The sweet smoky smell makes my stomach growl. "Dad's favorite. Scalloped potatoes, squash, coleslaw, and homemade mustard pickles."

"I'm starving." I pick away at the ham and try to avoid asking, but I have to know. "How is he?"

She slaps my fingers away. "Go on up and see—he's really tired from a sleepless night in the hospital. One side of his face is swollen and it's pretty colorful, but I don't think the fall did too much damage."

There's a wheelchair parked at the bottom of the stairs. A wheelchair? I take the stairs two at a time. "Hey, Dad—how're you doin'?" I look in through the bedroom door and make a face. "Oooo ... does your head hurt?"

"Not too bad, but I sure am glad to be home." He puts down his ice pack and pats the bed beside him. Hannah's already tucked in under his arm on the other side. "Smells a whole lot better here than there. Tell me about your day in the outside world."

I tell him about Roy and the little kids. "Everybody says he'll probably go to Waterton this time."

"Oh, swell. He can pick up a few pointers from the other crooks in there," he says. "I feel badly for the kids he scared."

"The brother of one of them is in my class," Hannah pipes up. "He says his baby brother won't even eat chocolate or chips anymore!"

Dad shakes his head, but he's grinning. "That's pretty serious. But I do feel sorry for Roy's mom, too. She's had a tough life from day one. Being a single mom and all."

"You coming down for supper?" I ask.

"Smells great—give me a hand, will you?"

I help him get out of bed and Hannah helps him put on his orange robe. He's so skinny, like a scarecrow without the stuffing. What's that scarecrow song Hannah's always singing? *"If I only had a brain ..."* Or, for Dad, a healthy brain.

"Or maybe I should get dressed," he says, after he ties the belt. "Do you think?"

Hannah wraps her arms around his waist. "I love your pumpkin robe."

"It's just us ... we don't care." I keep hold of his arm as we walk downstairs. He's shaky and hanging on tight to the banister on the other side.

"Might have to sleep on the couch for a while," he says, easing himself into the wheelchair. "Looks like I'll be stuck in this chariot for a while." I push him down the hall and into the dining room. "Good thing our old house has nice wide doorways."

The screen door bangs shut. "Hey, Dad." James drops his bag in the hall and bends down to give Dad a hug. "You okay? Nice wheels! Sorry I wasn't here last night."

Or the night before that, or the night before that ...

Dad laughs. "Well, you didn't miss much. Just your old man taking a tumble. But I'll be okay. You hungry?"

"Starving!"

"Dr. Crosby wants me to come in for another chest x-ray tomorrow," Dad says during supper. "He thinks there may have been a problem with the reading of the last one." He kind of drops it into the conversation between bites of ham, trying to act like it's no big deal. "He's looking into booking an appointment for me to have a CT scan, too."

"Maybe it's not in your lungs." Hannah leans over and presses her cheek into Dad's arm. "Maybe they made a boo-boo!"

"We can always hope." Mom doesn't look all that hopeful, but she smiles anyway. "More ham anyone? Coleslaw?"

"Got time for some one-on-one?" James flicks me with the towel while we're doing the dishes. Mom and Dad are watching the news and Hannah's upstairs singing.

I was going to work on *Hoop Heroes 4 Health* stuff all night, but since James never asks me to do anything, I say, "Sure. Let's go."

"You get first ball," he says, tossing it to me. "Remember the rockets."

I keep one eye on him and the other on the beat-up crooked rim above the shed door. Having my glasses back helps. But he's just so big. Every time I move, he's right on top of me, sticking to me like Velcro.

"Dig!" he says. "Keep your head up." Then he steals the ball and takes a shot. Perfect form.

I watch it bounce off the rim, then get myself in position for the rebound. He boxes me out, snags the ball out of the air way above my head, and rolls it in off his fingertips.

"You're too tall," I complain.

"But you're faster than me," he says. "More agile. You've got to play to your strengths."

Next shot he takes, I explode up the driveway, snag the rebound, protect the ball, dribble twice, then go in for a reverse layup.

"Whoa! Who taught you that little move?" He starts clapping.

"Joe," I say. Since you're never around.

"Not bad, Rocket Man. You're learning."

Rocket Man. I start humming the song. I remember the tune from the dance, but not the words.

Even though he takes it easy on me, he still slaughters me. "You're lookin' good, bro," he says, slapping me on the back. "Need some help with that Geezer game stuff?"

"We're trying to find the right group to give our money to—if there is any money," I say. "You could help me research a bunch of cancer charities."

"I already checked out your Web site—it's epic," he says, sitting down beside me at the computer. "How'd you figure out how to do all that tech stuff?"

"It's simple coding," I say. "Jeff did most of it, but I helped."

"The guys on my team are getting super pumped," James says. "And since we haven't lost so far this season, the Geezers will have their work cut out for them, even with Hank Jones."

"That's one thing I'm having trouble with—getting hold of Hank Jones. The TV business must keep a famous guy like him on the road."

"I'll ask around, see if anybody's got any connections."

I show him the digital image of Maria's poster. "We'll start putting them up around town next week."

"I like the biceps she gave me," James says, doing a body-builder pose. "But those tight booty shorts on the Geezers should be illegal, against the dress code. What else have you guys been doing?"

"Andy, Jeff, and me are basically living in the office at lunchtime, calling everybody who graduated from Oakdale in the past forty years," I tell him. "Which is mostly everybody in town over eighteen. One lady whose son was on Dad's team offered to do a display of old basketball pics for the lobby."

"Sweet. Wish I had more time to help."

Me, too.

"With all the bleachers pulled out, our gym's got about a thousand seats, plus some standing room. Should be lots of people around for the Christmas holidays. How great would that be if we could fill it?"

"You think ten dollars is too much for a ticket?" I ask.

He rolls his chair back and folds his hands together behind his head. "I think people will pay that, especially if we get Hank. Plus, you'll make money on the canteen."

"Jeff's mom's already got a freezer full of Whoopie Pies," I say. "It's not like we'll make millions but, hey, it's better than sitting around wishing we could help."

James leans forward and scrolls through the site. "*Hoop Heroes 4 Health* isn't exactly the most original name in the world."

I squint at him. "Got a better idea?"

He puts up both hands. "Chill. I'm just sayin'. But number four was Dad's jersey number, so it works."

"It's not blockbuster," I say, "but it's the best we could think of in a hurry."

He Googles *cancer charities* and gets thirteen million hits. "Whoa! This says there are 278 different cancer charities."

"Seriously?" I move in closer to the screen. "Let's pick one that's trying to find a cure."

"Well, cancer's been around for a few thousand years, and scientists today believe the best we can hope for is researching ways to prolong people's lives, help them live longer *with* cancer. An actual *cure* is pretty much impossible."

I read through the list. Lung cancer, colorectal, breast, pancreatic, sarcoma ... "Hey, that was Terry Fox's cancer— sarcoma ... bone cancer."

"Let's check out the charities specific to brain tumors," James says. "How about this one—the Brain Cancer Foundation?" He clicks on the link. "Let's read about what they do."

"Look at all the research grants they give out," I say. "That sounds good. Don't you think? And they've got lots of support groups, too. For people with brain tumors."

James nods and continues scrolling through the pages. "Yeah. It's perfect." He points at a picture. "Some of these guys doing the research don't look much older than me."

"Let's send them an email, tell them what we're doing," I suggest.

Dad's already in bed by the time we're done researching the Foundation and emailing them. Mom's knitting by the fire.

"G'night, Mom."

"Goodnight, Bobby—say a little prayer and keep your fingers crossed." She looks up and gives me a tired smile. "Don't let the bedbugs bite."

I drop my clothes on the floor, crawl into bed, and start thinking about God for some weird reason. I'm not too sure God's any more real than Santa Claus. I never thought much about him after I stopped going to Sunday school in Grade 4. My Grandma P. died that year. I did think lots about where she got to. Other than that big hole in the ground, I mean. Even when she was seventy, she used to swim across the lake every year. Somebody like that couldn't just disappear, could they?

I remember asking Mom why people get so stressed about death and what comes after. I mean, we didn't know what this life would be like 'til we got here, right? I close my eyes and have a silent chat with God, whoever and wherever he is. I guess that's what praying is. He doesn't answer me but I feel better after. And who knows? He might've been listening. Maybe he's got some amazing tech system where he's tapped into the brains of everybody in the whole world. And after all, even doctors make mistakes—sometimes ...

chapter thirteen

C heck it out! He was listening! I come home from school a few days later and Mom's all smiles. She even dances me around the kitchen a little. Dad's got pneumonia! Most families wouldn't be too stoked by that. But we're just happy the C Monster didn't decide to move his prickly self into Dad's lungs.

Dad's still pretty weak but, at least for pneumonia, there's a pill he can take. Dr. Crosby says he should be feeling a bit better within a few days.

"Let's order in Chinese food—to celebrate!" Mom suggests.

I look at her and grin. I can't remember the last time we did that.

"Yummy!" Hannah rubs her belly. She only likes fried rice and fortune cookies, which means me and James get to split her egg rolls, sweet and sour chicken balls, and wings. Sweet.

A few days later, Maria brings the finished poster to school—it's wicked. Coach is going to get both the D1 and D2 teams to put them up all around town. I'm freaking a little about getting hold of The Birdman, since his name's right there in extra-large bold print at the top of the poster: OAKDALE'S OWN SUPERSTAR. But time's running out—twenty-six days until December 27th.

Thing is, now we've gotta spill to Mom and Dad. We don't want them to find out by seeing a poster on some random bulletin board. Or do we? I can see them going for groceries and stopping to read the notice board like they always do. Looking for bargains. Maybe that is the way to go.

I call Joe after supper to see what he thinks. He jumps right in before I even say anything.

"He's in! I found him on Facebook, if you can believe an old farmer like me could figure out how to open a Facebook account. It's an amazing tool for finding people, I'll give it that. Hank says he'll plan his Christmas holiday around being here on the 27th. He still has family in the area. And, are you ready? Wait for it ... he says he might bring a couple of his former teammates with him!"

"Seriously? That would be amazing."

"Looks like things are really coming together for you, Bobby."

"For us, you mean. Wait 'til you see the sweet poster Maria made."

"Who's Maria? She that cute little thing I see with Hannah at the games?" Joe laughs.

"With the long hair?" I try to act like it's no biggie. "Yeah, that's her."

"She your girlfriend, your main squeeze?" he asks

"Huh?" That's the best answer I can come up with. Can't tell him I don't even know if she's my GF or not, can I?

"Hey ... did Mom tell you? Dad's only got pneumonia. His lung scan came back clear. I mean clear of cancer." My voice kind of breaks in the middle of cancer. I cough to cover it.

"Fantastic! I'm even more excited about the game now. Who knows ... maybe Rob'll be strong enough to play a few minutes by Christmas."

How freakin' epic would that be!

I spend an hour in the driveway, then go in to work on the game. Jeff helped me make a spreadsheet to organize all the people helping out—mothers baking sweets, kids working the canteen, D2 and D1, James's team, the Geezers, and their families. Coach said he'll run a 50/50 draw at halftime, and Mrs. Archibald said she'd put together a stage band. Coach Duncan from the Pee Wee league offered to set up a mini game as a halftime show. Parents love that cute kid stuff.

Oh, and then there's the cheerleaders. Franny Upton offered to be in charge of them now she's got some spare time on her hands, with Roy away and all. Plus, Hank Jones is her fifth cousin twice removed, or something like that. She probably thinks that makes her famous. She's so not the work-behind-the-scenes invisible type.

By the time I finish updating everything, it's like somebody's playing a bass drum in my head. It kind of freaks me out when I get a headache now. I've always had them but it's different now—with Dad's tumor.

"I'm wiped," I say to James. "I need sleep."

He looks up from his desk. "Me, too, but I've got this incredibly interesting History paper to finish—'Heartland and Hinterland in Canada.' Plus, I'm really starting to think about my science project. Oh ... and thanks, man." He leans over and gives me a fist-bump.

I look at my socks. "For what?"

"All the work you're putting into the game. Behind the scenes stuff. I'd never have taken on something like this when I was thirteen."

I shrug, like it's no big deal. "Well, see ya tomorrow." I can't think of anything else to say. King James telling me I did good? Me? That's a first. Maybe Mr. Invisible's becoming visible!

I brush my teeth real slow and stare at myself in the bathroom mirror. Is that just the light or ... I take my glasses off and lean in. No, it is! Check it out. There's a darkish shadow over my top lip. A 'stache. I rub my finger across it and look closer—and see an oozy white zit, right between my eyes. I blast the hot water, scrub my face hard, floss my teeth, then fall into bed.

I go to pack my bag for school and, guess what? No freakin' basketball shoes. I search the whole house—nothing. Must have left them at the gym after practice yesterday. The only other sneakers I have are skate shoes. Coach doesn't allow those on the basketball court. In fact, he says they shouldn't be allowed anywhere, anytime.

Soon as I get to school, I head straight to the gym and search everywhere: the locker room, under the benches, under the ping-pong tables on the stage. Hannah even checks the girls' locker room for me.

"I think I see them, Bobby," she shouts finally, from way up in the nosebleed section of the bleachers.

"Where?"

"At least, I think that's them." She points up. Way up.

All I can see are shreds of black cloth attached to rubber soles. Hanging from the steel beams in between a few escaped badminton birds.

"Great!" Those were Dad's lucky shoes—they're twenty-five years old, not that Roy would give a crap about a detail like that. I thought he was at Waterton; maybe he's just been hiding out at home, too embarrassed to come to school. As if.

"Heard today's Roy's court date," Jeff says when I meet him in the hall. "Hope he gets a nasty old judge, maybe the grandfather of one of those little kids."

"I wish." Then I tell him about the sneakers.

When we pass Roy's locker section, Kyle's there by himself. His father's on the school board. Must've talked the principal into letting Kyle come back to school. I give Kyle a mean squint, and he gives me a big ape grin back.

"Lose somethin', Blob?" He shoves me into a locker. "Maybe the cops can help you find them." Smells like he hasn't brushed his teeth in a month.

I shove him right back, which is way easier than I thought it would be. "It wasn't me that told," I say, "about Halloween. Wish it was, though."

"What're ya talkin' about? I didn't do nothin' with your messed-up shoes," he says, backing away.

I think like James and make myself tall. "You always this stupid, or you just tryin' extra hard today? Who said anything about shoes?"

Jeff and Andy lose it, start laughing like hyenas.

"What he said."

"Oooo ... harsh! Good one, Bobby."

Then we walk away, all slow and casual-like. Kyle's only a bit bigger than me, but fatter. I could probably seriously hurt him. Although, to be honest, I don't have a clue how to throw a punch. And I don't need any trouble. Plus, I'm pretty sure Roy put him up to it. The two of them put together might have one whole brain.

I get to my locker just before the bell. Great ... there's Franny Upton hanging around—again. What now?

"Hey, Bobby." She slouches back against my locker. I'm pretty sure what she's wearing is against the school dress code. The tight skirt barely covers her butt. She's got about ten of these big hula-hoop things poked through her ears, and her top's see-through, and she's wearing a lacey purple ...

I can feel myself turning red. "Hey." I try to get at my lock. Now would be a good time for Mr. Invisible to show up.

"How's the big game coming along?" Out of the corner of

my eye, I see her doing this weird pout thing with her lips. She looks like a codfish, kind of holding her mouth open. A codfish with bright red lips. I try not to laugh.

"Okay," I say. "Could I please get in my locker now—I'm gonna be late."

"Maybe I could show you the cheers we're working on sometime," she says, sliding out of the way. "Special cheers I made up, just for your game."

"Sure, we'll have a meeting and get everybody together," I say. "Soon."

"Here's my cell number. Call me anytime ... Bye-bye, Bobby ..." She giggles and wiggles off down the hallway.

I look up just in time to see Maria walking fast the other way. Sunny yellow ribbons. Only she doesn't look that sunny. In fact, she doesn't even say hi. This is not gonna be a good day.

There's a leaky pipe in the gym, so Coach cancels practice after school. Gives me some extra time to figure out what to do about my shoes.

I call Joe and tell him the problem.

"Let me buy you a new pair, Bobby ... or wait—I bet I still have my old Converse kicking around here someplace. They're exactly the same as Rob's, even the same size—we bought them together at Lane's Sporting Goods, back in the day."

"Nah, that's okay," I say. "I'll think of something."

"I want to help—it'd be great to see my old shoes in action again. They'd be a little snug on me now, with my gnarly old-man feet and my ingrown toenails."

"You sure? I sorta hate to tell Dad what happened to his. He doesn't need the stress."

"No need to. I'll swing by tonight. See you then."

"Anybody up for a walk?" Dad asks after supper. Mom's filling in for somebody at work and James has late practice. So we're enjoying Mr. Ragu's gourmet spaghetti again.

"Sure!" Me and Hannah both jump up from the table and grab our jackets. Hannah gets Dad his winter one. The poufy black one we got him for skiing one Christmas. When he used to come skiing with us.

Lucky we already got a wheelchair ramp built by the front door for when Gram was sick. It's a perfect night—tons of stars, and you can see little puffs of your breath. Hannah pretends she's blowing smoke rings. "Who am I?" she asks.

I shrug.

"Franny Upton ... I saw her smoking in the park after school today. Smoking's the stupidest thing in the whole world."

"Agreed," Dad says.

"Doesn't she know it causes cancer?"

The moon's massive and bright yellow when we start out. It shrinks as we walk slowly around the block and it gets higher in the sky. Rufus follows us, meowing and darting into the bushes. Chasing his shadow, probably. Or maybe he's hunting, like the summer he left a dead mouse on the front porch every morning. The paperboy must've thought we were freaky cult people.

"Night like this makes you glad to be alive, doesn't it?"

Dad holds his face up to the sky and breathes in deeply.

Hannah puts her hand in his and skips along beside the chair. She's humming like Mom.

We don't walk too far—Hank Jones is doing the NBA game on TV, and it's almost Hannah's bedtime. When we get back, Joe's sneakers are hanging on the front doorknob.

"What's this?" Dad holds them up. "Your shoes?"

"Oh ... um ..." I open the door and wheel him into the front hall. I don't want to tell him what happened. He's got enough to worry about. "I think ..."

"Did you forget them at the gym? Hey, wait a minute. These ones are all frayed at the top, and they smell like mothballs."

"Joe dropped them off for me to use," I say. "Your old ones ... um ... sort of got killed."

"How?" He wheels himself across the floor and turns on the kitchen light.

I shrug. "Somebody cut them up."

"Who ... and why?"

I shrug again. "I'm guessing Kyle and Roy—probably they're blaming me for telling the police about Halloween."

"Did you?" Dad asks, laying the sneakers on the table.

"No," I answer. "I did see them that night. I wondered what Roy was doing with a Pokémon pillowcase. I didn't see them doing the stealing, but I would've told on them if I did."

"Should I talk to their parents?" he asks.

"Daaad ..." I groan. "I'm not six years old anymore!"

He laughs. "Of course, you're not." He makes a fist and

gives me a little tap on the shoulder. "You'll soon be taller than me, especially since I'm shrinking. Sorry, little ... um ... I mean, big buddy."

I go upstairs and get out my science book. I've got a lab to do, but I get to thinking about when I *was* six years old, instead. Before I really became Mr. Invisible. Back then, all I did was have fun. That was my freakin' job. No homework, no jerks destroying my life, and—even better—no C Monster. My family used to laugh lots back then. Seemed like everything was a joke. I guess that's what adults mean when they say not to grow up too fast. The Family Studies teacher is always on about that. I'm starting to think she might know what she's talking about.

When I get stuck on the *Conclusions* part of the lab, I try on Joe's shoes, then do a few vertical jumps. Twice, all my fingers make contact with the ceiling. Barely, but still. The ten-foot ceiling. Sweet!

chapter fourteen

First person I see when I get to school a few mornings later is Roy, doing the rooster down my hallway. He stops to yank up his pants and check me into the lockers. "Blob, what's goin' down?" Turns out the judge put him on probation and gave him some community service work. I was so hoping he'd get put away for at least a few months—would all of Grade 8 be too much to ask for?

Coach calls me into his office after school. "Hey, Bobby ... can I talk to you for a second?"

"Sure." I drop my bag by the locker room. At least I got to play in a few D1 games. "What's up?"

"Any chance you could give Roy a hand with his community service work?"

I look at him like he sprouted horns. "Seriously? What do you mean?"

"I was thinking it might do him some good to work with the little kids in the Pee Wee program," he says. "You still do that, don't you?"

I try to make myself smile and say, "Sure," again. But I can't.

Guess Coach sees it on my face. "I know you and Roy aren't the best of friends," he says. "But it might be a chance for you to make a difference. Set a good example and all that. Take a leadership role."

"Well, I could try." I pick up my bag. Feels like somebody slipped some rocks into it when I wasn't looking. "He coming to practice today?"

"Not until he completes his community service." Coach winks. "You're in luck. You've been giving me lots of tough out there in practice. Keep it up. The Snowball Tournament's coming right up."

"Uh-huh." I pick up my bag and push the locker room door open with my shoulder. I don't feel all that lucky or tough.

Thursday after school, Roy's already at the gym when I get there. I notice right away that Brian's not there, the kid Roy terrorized, but the other little kids are all standing in a circle, watching Roy like he's some kind of NBA star. He charges in for a dunk, then starts doing the gorilla chin-ups. He's got a tattoo on his left bicep—FU, in big bold letters.

"Nice tattoo," I say. "Very friendly. Hope none of the kids ask what it means."

"Hey, Bobby!" he says, slapping me on the back. Like we're Batman and Robin or something. "Franny's initials ...

nice, eh?" Then his eyes go right to my shoes.

"Hey," I say. "Like my shoes? Nice, eh?"

He looks all confused and gets this stunned grin on his face. I don't bother to explain, just start cranking down the hoops. "So—what do we do?" he says, following me. The little kids are all running around us like ants. Soon as I blow the whistle, they line up under the end basket. That kind of power always makes me smile.

I get out my clipboard and show Roy a list of the stuff we're supposed to do. He looks at it hard, kind of squinting and rubbing his eyes. Then his face turns bright red. I don't get it.

"Simple, huh?" I ask. "Just games, really."

"Well, ummm ... the thing is ..." He's mumbling and I can hardly hear him. "Why don't you just tell me what to do?"

"You hang onto the list and make sure I don't forget anything," I say, picking up a ball. They're the mini ones, so I can palm it.

He twists his hat around to the side and looks down at his red shoes. "I can't read it."

I laugh. "As if."

He drills a ball into the floor about a hundred times, real fast.

"For real? You serious?" I wait for him to start snorting and strutting.

"Like I'd lie about it!" He picks up two balls and palms one in each hand. The little kids start hanging off his arms, trying to get at them. "Think I just hang out with the other dummies in the Resource Room for fun?"

Actually, I thought he was there keeping Franny company. "Well, no ... geez ... I didn't know. Forgot my crystal ball." I look away. "Anyway, the big thing is ... you gotta be nice to these kids. They're little—you can't drive the ball at them. You can't stuff them—you can't make them feel like crap!" I smile. I kinda like telling old Roy what to do. He doesn't even look quite so tall as he used to. "Why don't you start by cutting up those oranges for them to have at halftime."

Turns out the Pee Wees love him. He's funny and gets them laughing their crazy heads off by making freaky pigorilla faces. Takes some of the pressure off me, 'cause I'm really not that funny.

"Thanks, boys," Mr. Duncan says after the practice. "The kids loved having you two young guys here today. Hope you can both make it again on Saturday."

I look at Roy. He's looking at his scuffed-up shoes. "Sure," I answer. "We'll be here."

I follow Roy out of the gym. I figure now he's off-duty, he'll be back to his evil self.

"Hey, Bob ... thanks."

I stop walking and stare at him. Bob? Not Blob?

He kicks up some rotten leaves. His red shoes aren't so shiny anymore. He still smells like Christmas trees, though. "That was sort of decent."

"Hey ... no problem," I manage to spit out.

"Well ... catch ya later." He slams down his skateboard. Then, he grabs my Yankees hat and chucks it way up in a tree. He does a bunch of pig snorting, catches some air off the curb, then rides off before I even know what's going on.

"Idiot!" I drop my bag and start climbing up after my hat. That's so messed-up about him not being able to read. I might be evil, too, if it was me. School must seriously suck for him.

Mom and Dad are in a crazy good mood when I get home. They're cooking supper and singing along to some old country song on the radio. Something about Grandma's featherbed. One of Maria's posters is on the counter by the phone.

"Know anything about this?" Dad wheels over and picks it up.

"Ummm ... sort of." I look it over and grin. "James home yet?"

"Sorry—you're on your own." He smiles and reaches up to give me a big hug. I bend down and hug him back, just a little. Well, really, my arms stay at my sides, but my face touches his.

I explain it all to them. "Tons of people are helping. Didn't anybody tell you? Joe even got Hank Jones to come."

"I can't believe you did all that ... mostly on your own," Dad says. "According to Joe."

"We're so proud of you, Bobby." Mom gives me another hug.

"Guess I better get myself whipped into shape," Dad says, taking an air shot. "A little one-on-one after supper? I'm allowed out of the chair for a little bit, so long as I don't overdo it."

"Okay," I say. "Yeah! I can show you my new rockets."

It's weird how every week is so totally different. Last week, everything was brutal. Today—it's all good. And Mr. Invisible might be gone—for good.

December 20th! I look at the calendar and start to freak. There's still way too much to do.

Maria comes over in the afternoon. We're still making phone calls. The girls' basketball team's been helping her with calling, and we're up to "т" in the phonebook.

"Hi, Mr. Thorsen. No, no, I'm not a telemarketer." I give Maria a shrug and mouth, "Are we?" Then I go on. "I'm calling from Oakdale School, and we're looking for basketball fans. The Celtics?"

Maria starts waving at me. "Eastern Travel donated a trip to Boston for a Celtics game," she whispers, showing me the prize booklet. "Tell him."

"Yes, Mr. Thorsen. Great team, the Celtics, and one of our door prizes is a trip for two to Boston to catch a game. Anyway, we're organizing a basketball game on December 27th. The high school team from 1982 versus this year's team. The tickets are only $10. Yes, sir ... it's called *Hoop Heroes 4 Health*, and we're raising money for The Brain Tumor Foundation. Two tickets? Sweet. We'll put them aside for you at the door. Thank you."

Maria high-fives me. "You're a pro. My turn."

"What are we forgetting?" When we're finished calling, I scroll down through the spreadsheet. "I talked to the guy at the hospital yesterday, and he's good to go."

James comes in and starts reading over my shoulder.

"What's the hospital got to do with the game?" he asks.

I close the window and keep my eyes on the screen. "Did I say hospital? I meant ... um ... the print shop. We ordered a few more posters."

"Did you get a chance to check out Franny's cheerleaders yet?" Maria pokes me with her elbow.

"They know it's a family event, right?" James says. "No boobs or butts?"

"Least she's not hanging out at my locker anymore. Now Roy's back and all," I say. "And that's a *real* good thing."

Me and old Roy are still working with the Pee Wees. We're even doing a Family Studies project together: *Team Means* T.*ogether* E.*veryone* A.*chieves* M.*ore*. Surprisingly, Roy can draw decent cartoons, which is awesome, since I draw like a five-year-old. Mr. Duncan even persuaded Brian to come back, but he still keeps his distance from Roy, even though Roy's way better than me at the fun stuff. The little kids love him swinging them around and showing off. But they still line up when I blow my whistle.

Last week, Coach let Roy start practicing with the team again.

"Think we'll go with eleven men this season," he said, after Roy's first day back. Then he looked at me. "If you're available, Bob?"

I just grinned. Don't know how much floor time I'll get, but at least I'm *really* on the D1 roster—finally. Plus I'll get to play in the big Snowball Tournament this weekend. The funny thing is Roy totally doesn't seem that tall anymore.

Maybe it's because he gave up the rooster strut. He stopped shaving his head a while back, too.

Mom measured me the other day. She wrote it on the wall: just under five foot eight. Explains why I'm always crashing into corners and banging into the furniture. I'm taller than Andrews now. For some strange reason, I think he likes the new me better than Mr. Invisible. I was two minutes late for math yesterday and he didn't say a word. I haven't started shaving—yet. But there's a shadow there, a real orange shadow.

"How's this look, Bobby?" Hannah asks. She and her friends are making thank-you cards for each of the Geezers and the Rookies. Maria's going to put her Photo-shopped team pictures in with the cards.

"Awesome, Hannah—they'll love those!" Maria says. Pink ribbons today.

"Anybody interested in popcorn?" Mom asks.

"Oh, yeah!"

"Mmmm … mmmm!" Dad wheels in behind her with a big bowl of popcorn on his lap. "Organic and buttery! Anybody for some delicious wheat grass juice to wash it down?"

He goes to this naturopath lady now. She's got him making juice out of some pretty sketchy stuff. Seems more like cow feed. Maria talks to him by the hour about all that granola food, and her mother's always sending over sugar-free muffins and cookies, stuff cancer cells don't like.

Even though he's over the pneumonia, Dad's still kind of dizzy, and Dr. Crosby says he should keep using the chair, just until they figure out what the C Monster's up to. He says the balance thing might only be from his fall. I wish.

I check the lists again after Maria leaves. The one thing I forgot—Christmas! Guess I better hustle my butt out to the mall. Last year, I gave everybody coupons. Two hours of theater practice for Hannah, a season's pass to my games for Dad and James, and a pot of Bob's Blend for Mom ... my secret recipe: hot dogs, noodles, dill pickles, and liquid cheese. Come to think of it, she never did cash in that coupon. Maybe I'll just go for chocolate this year. I wonder if Maria likes Turtles?

chapter fifteen

"How're the new shoes working out?" Dad asks. "Not as comfortable as my old ones," I say. "But they'll do." Mom and Dad got me new shoes at Lane's the other day. An early Christmas present. Sweet blue Nikes with little flames on the ankles. My rockets. They're almost as sweet as the flashing dinosaur sneakers I had when I was six. They're bringing me good luck so far. Two games into the Snowball Tournament and I've already scored eighteen points—ten more than I scored all last season.

"All set?" Mom asks. "Your uniform's clean and I put an extra pair of socks in your bag. Did you remember your deodorant?"

"Sweet." I start digging through my bag, making sure

Joe's sneakers are there for back-up. "Hang on a sec."

"Wait for me," James yells down from upstairs.

"You're coming?" I say.

He skips the bottom three steps, lands at my feet, and punches my shoulder. "Wouldn't miss this for anything. I'm psyched—my little bro, playing point guard in the Snowball final? I need to see what you've got if you're going to play with us big boys in the Hoop Heroes game."

"Got some deodorant I can borrow?" I ask.

"Sure, no sweat," James says. "I'll just grab it upstairs."

Then we look at each other and fist-bump across the banister. "Pun!" we say together. "No sweat!"

"Should I get my pom-poms?" Hannah asks.

I shake my head and stuff a finger down my throat like I'm gagging.

She giggles. "Kidding—I'm way past pom-poms. That was so last year."

"Look at the cars. Must be something else going on at the school," I say when we get there. The parking lot's almost full. My game-gut snakes start wiggling.

"Maybe all the publicity around *Hoop Heroes 4 Health* helped," Dad says.

"Hey, Rocket Man," James says. "Think you'll use some of the tricks I've been showing you?"

"That's the plan." Rocket Man. Now that's a name I could get used to. Sorry, Mr. Invisible.

James and me cleaned all the snow off the driveway and practiced for an hour and a half last night. "You've gotta be able to see every player in only two or three strides," he told me. "A guard's got to be as good at passing with his left hand as he is with his right, and you've got to make your move fast—especially when you're looking for a fast break." Took two hours to get the feeling back in my fingers after we were done.

The stands are already half full when we get inside, even though it's an hour before game time. We're used to having twenty or thirty people at our middle-school games, max. Good thing I'm not still looking to be Mr. Invisible. I grin up at Maria while I'm waiting my turn to shoot in the warm-up.

Before we break from our huddle, Coach tells us we've got a new team mantra. "FAST," he says. "It works real good with 'BREAK.'" We shout "FAST," then clap hands for "BREAK," and the starters hit the floor.

I keep saying it over and over again in my head while we wait for the tip-off. *Fast Break … Fast Break … Fast Break …*

Roy wins the toss and passes it back to me. I start down the floor and look up to see who's open. I fake right, then turn and pass the ball left to Luke. He spins, then passes it in to Kyle. He dribbles twice, goes up, and … scores! We're first on the board—hope that's a good sign.

At halftime, the score's tied at 38. Roy's already got three fouls. Coach has to keep him off until we really need him. "Luke and Kyle … you've gotta give Bob somebody to pass to. He can't do it all alone."

Second half starts off slow. I take a couple of foul shots; the first one goes in; the second one goes wild off the rim. A Millwood guy picks up the rebound and drills the ball to their end. Number 5's hanging in the key. He grabs it and drops it in.

"Box out!" Coach shouts. "That was your rebound, Prescott."

We get the ball back and I carry it over half. I look up and see Kyle dancing around right under the basket. *Fast break ... fast break ... fast break ...* I put his name on the ball and send it, baseball-style. It goes right into his hands and he tips it in.

"Nice one, Bobby. Keep it up!" Coach yells. "Push hard."

The game gets real fast after that. I signal for a water break. Roy takes my place.

"Stay out of foul trouble," Coach warns him. "Hands to yourself."

I sit down on the bench next to the little kid wearing the Oakley the Owl costume. He hoots at me, then pats me on the back with one wing.

"You're looking good out there," Coach says to me as I'm sucking back some water. "You're fast ... play to your strength. Don't let them shut you down. Kyle's staying open under the basket. Look for your options and don't be afraid to take an outside shot yourself."

Roy gets a three-pointer, practically from half, then comes back off. He's still only got three fouls with four minutes to play. He's our best scorer. I hope Coach puts him back in real quick.

I carry the ball over half and get wedged into the lane. I stop dribbling but I'm caught. I twist all around, protecting the ball, trying not to fall over the line, looking for somebody that's open. Anybody. Luke's dancing around behind his Millwood guy. I reach around and hook him a bounce pass. He grabs it and drives to the hoop.

Millwood's ahead 58 to 56. Ninety seconds on the clock. Coach gives me the signal for full-court press and sends Roy back in. We've got to shut down number 5; he's their scoring machine. And I'm on him. I run backwards and sideways like a crazy person. Keep my eyes on his feet as he carries the ball into their end. I'm in his face, poking, trying to force the play. He stops dribbling. I've got him! I jab away at the ball like a boxer. Finally, I poke it free. Roy grabs it on the scramble and heads to the basket.

The defender gets a piece of it and Roy's shot goes off the backboard; number 5 snags it. He's quick. I blast over to him. He tries to pass, but I block it and catch the deflection. I protect the ball and he finally gives me some space. I look over the floor, see an opening, then take off dribbling. The crowd starts counting down the clock.

"*Ten ... nine ... eight ... seven ...!*"

I fake a pass to the right, then dribble into the key. Number 5's all over me again like Dr. Octopus. I keep low, dribble right, then pivot left and up. He fouls me, but it's in! My first buzzer beater. The crowd loses it. Never thought I'd hear so many people yelling my name. "Way to go, Prescott! Bobby, Bobby, he's our man ..."

The whole gym goes quiet as I step up to the foul line. I glance over at the clock. Three seconds. This is it. Oakdale Middle hasn't won the Snowball in fifteen years. I drill the ball into the floor. One, two, three times. I position my hands on the ball, just the way Dad taught me, and look up at the basket. You can do this, I tell myself. Just like you've done it a thousand times before. I bend my knees, go up on my toes, and let it go. The ball floats out of my hands like it knows right where it's going. *Swish.* The crowd starts chanting. *Oakdale! Oakdale!* The ref passes me back the ball. I take a deep breath and put my toe on the line. I tune out the crowd so all I can hear is my heart pounding. The arc looks good, but the ball rolls around the rim, then drops out. But that's okay. The buzzer goes. The game's over. Final score: Oakdale 59, Millwood 58!

Everybody jumps up off the bench, hooting and hollering, slapping me on the back, and high-fiving me. Even Roy gives me a full-body chest slam. Maybe he'll switch to football when he gets to high school.

"Good aggression out there, Prescott," Coach says. "Not bad for a D1 rookie."

When I come out of the locker room, people are still hanging around. All the way down the hall, people I don't even know are saying stuff to me and Dad.

"Good game, Bobby."

"Nice shooting, Bobby—good to see you got the Prescott basketball genes from your old man."

"Way to take charge of the floor, kiddo." (That was Joe.)

"Wicked game, Rocket Man!" (James.)

By the time I get in the back seat with Maria, I'm grinning so big, I can't remember why I ever wanted to be Mr. Invisible.

chapter sixteen

"*Go Bobby! Bobby, Bobby ... he's our man ...*"
I get a breakaway; tied game, two seconds on the clock.
"*Slurp ... Slurrrrp!*"
What the ...?

"Rebound—go away! Off!" I push him away, then stuff my head under the covers. And then I remember. It's December 27th. And last night we got word that Hank and his friends are stuck in the city in a blizzard that's coming our way. People better understand it's not our fault. But why did we put his name in such big print on the posters?

Rebound barks and starts tugging on my quilt. Seems Bailey was getting pudgy because she found herself a boyfriend on one of her escapes; Rebound's one of her puppies. Hannah wanted to call him Toto, since he was her Christmas present, but we talked her out of it. We're all hoping he'll grow up to be a perfect dog, like his mother—someday. So far, he's a chocolate-eating, garbage-digging, shoe-chewing, evil demon. Our new mantra is, "At least he's cute."

I tune in to the weather channel as soon as I get up. I've been glued to it, like, 24/7 for a week; I'm practically a meteorologist. They're calling for a wicked storm sometime in the next twenty-four hours, but they're not being real specific.

Except for the weather, *Hoop Heroes 4 Health* is looking good—healthy, you could say. I'm catching on to this pun thing. We've sold tons of tickets, not the whole thousand, but lots.

"Let's go, James—we gotta get to the gym." On my way downstairs, I bang on his door, then open it. He grunts and rolls over with his back to me.

We get there just before ten o'clock. About twenty people are already there. Maria and her decorator friends are putting up streamers and balloons. Jeff and Andy are folding programs. Some mothers are setting up the canteen in the hallway by the trophy case. I stop to look at the Snowball Cup and the other big basketball trophy in the center of the case. I lean in closer and try to find the little plaque with Dad's name on it. There it is, right in the middle: *Rob Prescott, MVP, 1981-82.*

"Hey!" Maria's arms are full of balloons, rainbow colors like her ribbons. "Are you excited, or what?"

"I guess so—but my stomach's not that great." James

finally persuaded me I should play tonight, and the snakes are having a party in my gut already. I mean, a thousand people? "Did you hear Hank and those guys can't get here?"

"It'll be okay," she says. "People didn't really buy tickets just to see The Birdman play, anyway."

"Maybe not, but for sure there'll be some people that are pissed."

By the time we head home for supper, the snow is seriously starting to pile up. The wind's howling, whipping the snowdrifts into mountains. Mom made my favorite—pizza—but the extra pepperoni's not settling real well in my stomach.

The roads are icy when we head back to the gym just after five. You can see maybe a foot in front of the van, like we're driving straight into a white wall. We slide around the corner by the high school and James almost goes off the road. But not because it's slippery; there are dozens, no, hundreds, of people lined up under the overhang outside the gym! I've never seen so many people in one spot in Oakdale before. Even with the wicked storm. My heart starts pounding, but it's all good.

"Phone for you, Bobby," Maria says as soon as I get inside.

"We've gotta get the doors open. Did you see all those people freezing out there?" I take the phone from her. "Hello?"

"Hey, Bobby. It's Hank Jones."

"Hey … you sound just like on TV." Hank Jones! I'm talking to The Birdman on the phone—can you believe it?

"I'm at the Maple Ridge train station. They just announced

they're shutting down all the trains, and I can't get a cabbie that's willing to travel that far. Can somebody pick me up? It's just me ... my buddies didn't want to risk the weather."

Maple Ridge is fifteen minutes away. What idiot would go that far in this weather?

"What's your number? I'll call you right back." I scribble the number on my hand, hang up, then stand by the outside gym door and watch the snow piling up against the fence around the soccer field. Hank's so close. There's gotta be a way to get him here.

I'm thinking hard when I hear a loud rumbling. Somebody's zigzagging across the soccer field on a snowmobile. I grin and watch him strut across the parking lot.

"Hey, Roy. Wanna do me a big favor?"

At six-thirty, we hit the floor and start warming up. People are streaming into the stands and the buzz in the crowd is wicked. My ears are ringing. You'd think this was the NBA playoffs. I keep one eye on the door. Roy looks like some kind of ice man when he finally blows in, grinning like crazy and pumping one fist in the air.

A few minutes later, the locker room door flies open and Hank Jones flies out. He charges in for an awesome between-the-legs dribble, reverse slam-dunk, his signature shot. I'm pretty happy to see him. And I'm not the only one. Everybody starts stomping and clapping, whistling and screaming. Coach can barely get the crowd to settle down when it's time to start. The mayor blabs on for a bit, then he passes the microphone to me. I hold it hard so my hands won't shake. Where's Mr. Invisible when I need him?

"Hey, everybody. Um ... thanks for coming out on such a stor ... stormy night." My voice cracks on "stormy." I clear my throat and wish I had notes. Public speaking is so not what I do for fun. I look at James sitting on the bench. He's grinning and nodding, so I keep going.

"Um ... lots of people have done lots of work on *Hoop Heroes 4 Health*. Most of their names are in the program. I just want to mention one, um ... my dad, Rob Prescott. We all wouldn't be here tonight—well, especially Hannah, James, and me—if it wasn't for him. Well ... him and my mom."

Everybody laughs.

I swallow hard and keep going. "My dad's a tough guy, and ... well ... he's my hero. My hoop hero." I put down the microphone, walk over to the Geezers' bench, bend down, and give him a hug. Talk about PDA ...

The band starts playing, and Hannah gets up to sing the anthem. She closes her eyes and sings her face off. My throat gets all dry and lumpy; I bug my eyes open to keep them from getting watery. I glance over at Dad in his wheelchair. Tears are pouring down his face. In the front row, Mom looks like she's about to burst.

They announce the starting lines. Me, James, and Dad are all starting. Well, Dad's an honorary starter. He's in his chair, playing left bench ... so far. We all get in a huddle and the crowd goes wild. I mean, seriously wild. Mega-PDA! I even see Joe wiping away at his eyes.

The ref blows his whistle and goes to center. Everybody's ready. Then, instead of getting in position, all the Geezers, except for Dad, line up single-file, and march out through the main gym doors.

chapter seventeen

James looks at me and mouths, "What's going on?" The crowd goes all quiet for a few seconds, then everybody starts whispering. Sounds like a hornet's nest. Feels like all 2,000 eyes are looking at me, wondering what's going on. I just grin and wait for it.

The doors open again and it's like a Remembrance Day parade. Each Geezer is sitting in a wheelchair, pushing an empty one in front of him. For the Rookies. I look at Joe, and he's grinning like he just won the lottery, trying to wheel his chair and push one at the same time. They all give Dad a high-five when he comes out to join the starters, and we hit the floor as the crowd goes wild.

Playing basketball in a wheelchair is epic. I mean, you wouldn't think so, but it's fun. Not easy, though, when you don't know how to steer the thing. Steering, wheeling, shooting, and passing, all at the same time. I don't know how the wheelchair players do it. Not that I'm saying it's better than regular ball, but it's still pretty sweet once you catch onto it. It's a lot like bumper cars. Old Roy would be a natural.

Dad plays defense on me. Amazingly, I score once from almost the top of the key. I think he let me. He's good, even in the chair. But then, he's got more experience than the rest of us. The ref doesn't bother to make many calls, since nobody's doing intentional fouls, more just trying to keep the ball in play. The Geezers are ahead by five when the buzzer goes at halftime.

The Pee Wees have a little scrimmage, and Franny and her cheerleaders put on an okay halftime show. By that I mean they don't look totally stupid. They keep it decent, anyway. Hank comes out and does a few Globetrotter-style tricks. Then Mom and a bunch of other mothers run out of the locker room. Some of their old cheerleader outfits are a little tight, but they get the crowd roaring. It's like seeing my parents in a flashback to the 1980s—with a few more gray hairs. Totally intense!

We play the second half without the chairs. It's not quite as funny, but still fun. With two minutes left, and the Rookies ahead by ten, Coach pretends to trip over the cord. The clock goes black, and the score disappears. The crowd freaks. We play for a few more minutes, shake hands, and Coach declares it a tie.

When the standing O is over, Dad wheels up to the

microphone. He looks good. Strong. Guess the C Monster is chillaxin' at home.

"It's my turn to say thanks, I guess." He claps in the direction of the fans. "To all of you, especially for coming out in this blizzard. What an amazing evening—there's already been some talk of making this an annual event. May *Hoop Heroes 4 Health* have a long and ..." he glances over at me ... "excuse the pun, healthy life."

He waits for the applause to die down.

"As most of you know, my younger son, Bobby, is the brains and the brawn behind tonight. He said earlier that I was his hero. To me, a hero is somebody you look up to, somebody you admire, somebody who's brave and outstanding. Well, I can tell you, I couldn't be prouder of Bobby. He's my hero, my superhero, and I plan on sticking around for a long time, just to see what he'll do next. Thank you, and good night."

My throat's all dry and fuzzy. I tip up my water bottle and chug. Dad wheels over and shakes my hand. I blink about a million times. Then I swallow about another million times. I will not cry, I will not cry, not in the gym in front of Roy and a thousand other people. And I don't.

Hank pulls the cord, and a thousand purple and gold balloons float down from the ceiling. I see Maria making her way through the people and the balloons toward me. Purple and gold ribbons.

I wrap my arms around her and we kiss. I mean, really kiss. I even close my eyes.

"Hey, Bobby, sweet job." Roy's got his arm around Franny

and he's grinning. "How much money did ya make?"

"Your timing sucks, Roy. Totally." But I grin. "We didn't count the money yet, but I'll let you know. And, hey ... thanks for picking up Hank."

"Hey, no problem. He and my mom had a thing back in the day. He's comin' over for supper tomorrow night. Says he'll teach me a few tricks."

"Sweet. See ya at practice."

After the crowd clears out, me and my family head for the door.

"Goldilocks and the four bears," Hannah says, putting on her hat. "That old blizzard can't hurt us. We're not scared of nothin'. Not even the nasty old C Monster."

We all laugh and head out into the storm. It's all good— for the Rocket Man!

Acknowledgments

All kids need a little help, a little hope and somebody who believes in them.
- Magic Johnson

Since I'm still a kid in the writing world, this quote from Bobby's hero, Magic Johnson, seems an apt way to begin my thank-you notes.

Thank you to my Head Coach, Peter Carver, for believing in me, for his wise guidance and patient handling of niggling issues during the editing of this book, and for getting me off the bench and giving me lots of playing time on the floor! And thank you to the entire Red Deer / Fitzhenry & Whiteside team for your behind-the-scenes work in getting my books into the hands of readers.

I'm forever grateful to volunteers who spend countless

hours as coaches and organizers of kids' sports; this work is so incredibly important in the lives of kids and their families. In particular, thank you to the late Sandy Allen of Truro, and the Sheriko family of Wolfville, who facilitated Wolfville Minor Basketball for so many years while learning to live with cancer in their family.

As always, thank you to my parents, Bob and Ada Mingo, both of whom were taken by the C Monster far too early—you're still here with us, every day, in so many ways.

Thank you to the many middle-grade novelists, especially Kate DiCamillo, whose books inspire me to continue working hard at my craft.

And to librarians, independent booksellers, teachers, and readers—without you, I couldn't be a writer; thank you for that privilege.

Hugs to my friends and family, especially my starting line-up—Don, Liam, Shannon, and Charlie, who, on a daily basis, put up with my living simultaneously in two worlds. You are my All-Stars, forever and ever.

Interview with Jan Coates

What was the first spark for this story?

The impetus for this story came from the Sheriko family, who facilitated Wolfville minor basketball for many years while living with cancer in their midst. The Sherikos eventually began a summer camp in Prince Edward Island specifically for kids living with chronic illness in the family. I'll be sharing a portion of my royalties from this book with Camp Triumph, the mission statement of which is: "to acknowledge, support, and provide an opportunity for children and youth, whose families are affected by chronic illness or disability, by building confidence and positive self-esteem through modeling, perseverance, respect, and understanding."

My parents both lived with cancer for many years before

their premature deaths, so I have some personal experience with the "C Monster" as well. And I have a soft spot for kids who love sports and play with heart, but who aren't necessarily the best players.

There are a number of compelling themes in this story but which one would you most like your readers to focus on?

When people ask what the book is about, I typically say "basketball," but really this is a story about a boy who loves his family and basketball, discovering that there are different ways of becoming a "hero," through hard work, drive, and determination.

Bobby needs, above all, to gain self-confidence as his story opens. What do you think is the key that opens the door for him?

Something I've learned as a parent over the years is that motivation and desire are sometimes even more important than ability in many areas—academic, leadership, artistic, or athletic pursuits. I didn't know that when I was a kid. I believed it was only the people who were born with certain talents who achieved excellence. So for Bobby, it's his desire—both to play basketball and help in his dad's struggle with cancer—that gives him the confidence to succeed. Well, that, and the hours he puts in practicing basketball and organizing *Hoop Heroes 4 Health*.

You like to catch the voices of young people in your dialogue. How do you know about that?

Quite honestly, I'm a shameless eavesdropper. Whenever I'm around young people, I listen closely, and I also ask people with kids the age of my characters to share any expressions they hear their kids using a lot. I do a lot of reading out loud when I'm writing, trying to see if the dialogue sounds "real." I suppose reading other middle grade novels is also a source I use for hints about writing realistic dialogue. I wish I had middle-grade readers available to proofread my books, but I don't since my own kids are in their twenties now.

Roy is the bad guy in the story—and yet in the end he's changed. What does that say about the nature of bullies and bullying?

When my kids were younger, I spent a lot of time explaining to them that kids are often mean because of unfortunate circumstances in their lives beyond their control. In Roy's case, his mom is on her own and has addiction issues, and he also has learning difficulties. Bullies aren't born that way—over time, they become unhappy people who struggle to raise their own self-esteem by belittling other people. It's hard for kids to understand this when they're constantly being harassed or bothered by "mean" kids, but being advised to look for the story behind the bully's behavior helps develop empathy in young people. I don't believe anybody, especially a kid, is predestined to be a bully for life. Sometimes, the right friend or the right activity (in Roy's case, helping with the Pee Wee team) at the right time can make all the difference.

Have you been, and are you now a basketball player— and were/are you on the D1 team?

Sadly, no, I've never played basketball, but I've always enjoyed watching the game. It's one of the few sports I actually understand fairly well! I've been a badminton player all my life, and I played competitive badminton between the ages of fourteen and twenty, so any understanding I have of involvement in sports comes from that experience, and from watching my own kids play soccer and basketball.

Participating in sports, both organized and recreational, helps kids become stronger and develop in so many ways—problem-solving, social and leadership skills, self-discipline, work ethic, cooperation, and learning to focus, as well as the obvious health benefits of physical fitness. I wish all kids could have the opportunity to enjoy playing sports regularly.

What advice would you give young writers about where to find stories?

When I visit schools, I always encourage young writers to be nosey. Every single day there are things happening under your very nose that could provide the seeds of a great story. Use your imagination and ask, "What if?" Fiction is a wonderful thing in that the writer is in complete control of the characters' lives in his/her story—the kind of control most kids dream of one day having over their own lives!

Thank you, Jan.